THE WIFE'S SILENCE

AMANDA MCKINNEY

Storm
PUBLISHING

Ebook ISBN: 978-1-80508-890-5
Paperback ISBN: 978-1-80508-891-2

Cover design: Lisa Horton
Cover images: Arcangel, Shutterstock

Published by Storm Publishing.
For further information, visit:
www.stormpublishing.co

Buried Deception

Trail of Deception

Broken Ridge

The Viper

Mad Women

The Raven's Wife

The Widow of Weeping Pines

Berry Springs

The Woods

The Lake

The Storm

The Fog

The Creek

The Shadow

The Cave

Black Rose Mystery

Devil's Gold

Hatchet Hollow

Tomb's Tale

Evil Eye

Sinister Secrets

Standalones

Lethal Legacy

For Mama and Henry

PROLOGUE
EMILIA

I stand naked in front of the bathroom mirror. My white-blonde hair is limp and greasy, tucked behind my ears. Candlelight flickers across a pale, gaunt face. I don't recognize the woman staring back at me. The sallow skin, the dark, hollow eyes.

I try to remember the woman before this, but she is so far gone, she's nothing more than a distant memory.

My grip tightens around the pill bottle, as if it's the only thing anchoring me to this moment, to anything. I feel out of my body, like I'm unmoored, drifting through this weird time-space without a sense of direction.

One handful, I tell myself. One handful and it will all stop. The noise. The crushing weight. The suffocating darkness.

I twist the cap off the bottle, the plastic clicking against the stillness of the room. I am eerily calm, unfeeling even in my own skin. The pills rattle inside the bottle, a soft, almost mocking sound. These tiny white fragments of fate—so simple and unassuming, yet capable of ending everything. Something I was too weak to do so long ago.

My gaze shifts to the porcelain bathtub, to the streaming water gently swirling in the tub. Beckoning me.

When I turn back to the mirror, I'm startled by a sudden voice. *His* voice. Muted, distant, like he's calling to me from underwater.

"Emilia?"

I flinch, the calmness inside me instantly evaporating. The sound of my name, the concern in his tone, hits like a stab to the chest. I don't want him to see me like this.

"Are you okay?" His voice is softer now, a haunting sing-song tone.

No. He can't see me like this.

Panic shoots up my spine, sending my pulse flying.

"What are you doing?"

My hand, clutching the pill bottle, begins to tremble as I stare at my reflection. My ugly, sad, pitiful face.

"Do you want me to leave you alone?"

Alone.

Tears fill my eyes. I've felt nothing but alone... for how long now? An eternity. This hollow ache in my chest, this emptiness that has consumed me.

I don't answer. I can't. The words get stuck in my throat.

Breathe, Emilia.

I close my eyes, focusing my awareness on the water in the tub, on the steady rhythm as it fills to the top. I take a deep breath. Then another. And then—he's gone. The voice that lingers in the shadows of my mind. Always there. Always reminding me of the past.

I suck back the tears, refusing to let them out. Refusing to fall apart again.

Before I can stop myself, I toss back the pills and chug the water.

Relief comes hard and fast.

I did it.

It's done.

A flutter of emotions ripple through me as I turn to the bathtub and take the first step into the unknown.

ONE

Now

Lightning slashes the midmorning sky as my Tahoe crawls up a long driveway that weaves through dozens of meticulously trimmed trees. It reminds me of a park.

I release a low whistle. "They are *rich*," I mutter, taking it all in.

The property sits on a mountain peak and stretches across a rolling manicured lawn with unobstructed views of the Chattahoochee-Oconee National Forest.

When the home comes into view, my jaw drops. Even through the curtain of rain, it's stunning. Muted colors and blurred landscape reflect against walls of sweeping windows. Windows, *everywhere*. A house made of glass, dissolving the boundary between the inside world and the outside one. A massive American flag hangs from one of the peaks, whipping in the rain.

As I approach, the reflection shimmers with changing hues of gray and brown. Instead of feeling fragile—considering all the glass—the home exudes a looming, strong presence. The sharp lines and reflective exterior stick out like sore thumbs in the lush vegetation. It seems to invade the nature around it, like a war tank bulldozing through a field of delicate flowers. It doesn't fit.

Still, it's beautiful and I cannot believe I will be working here—*living here*—for the foreseeable future.

When I saw the post for a live-in nanny, I thought, *bingo*. Finally, an opportunity to move out of my car. I hadn't expected to be caring for a sixty-three-year-old stroke victim instead of a child—a detail Mr. Caine had conveniently saved for our final phone interview. But after months of sleeping in my Tahoe, I wasn't about to get picky about the specifics.

At the top of the drive, I brake, unsure if I should park in front of the five-car garage or under the porte cochere. I choose the porte cochere, considering the thunderstorm raging overhead. Changing seasons are brutal in the South, especially during springtime.

The Tahoe sputters as I turn off the engine. I glance at the clock—9:42 a.m. I'm early.

Nerves tickle my stomach. I will them to go away. *This is the plan*, I remind myself. This is the first day of the rest of my life.

Pocketing my keys, I climb out of the SUV and close the door.

I immediately notice the lack of noise, aside from the deluge overhead. No cars, no trucks, no sirens, horns, or voices. The home is truly out in the middle of nowhere, surrounded by miles of wilderness.

I run my palms over the black slacks I purchased for half off at a thrift store the day before. With them, I've paired a conservative white button-up that I picked up at a homeless shelter a few months earlier. My new boss didn't mention a dress code, but I thought it prudent to bring my A-game on the first day. Especially considering how much he's paying me.

I smooth my brown hair, my fingertips lingering on the wiry

gray hair I found this morning. I make a mental note to pluck it as soon as I get settled. (Rich people don't like gray hair, right?) Then, I reposition the thick black framed glasses that have slid to the tip of my nose.

The smell of wet earth and pine fills the air as I reach the front door. It has a long, angular handle and a beveled window that allows for distorted views inside.

I ring the doorbell. A fancy chime echoes through the interior. I recognize it as "The Stars and Stripes Forever". The song that always plays on the Fourth of July. *Weird.* I glance up at the American flag hanging from one of the tall eaves. A patriotic family, then. Noted.

A minute passes, then another.

When I ring the bell again, a flash of movement appears behind the glass. The door swings open.

"I'm sorry," the man apologizes, having obviously come from his home gym. Despite his salt-and-pepper hair, he moves with an energy that belies his age. His white T-shirt and gray jogging shorts cling to a ridiculously shredded body; clearly, this is a man who refuses to surrender to time.

"Lucy Greer, right?" He smiles widely, but then tilts his head and studies me in a way that makes me shift my weight. But I'm used to this. It's not every day you meet someone with two different-colored eyes. And mine, well, they are as extreme as it gets. One is dark brown, almost black, and the other is ice blue. Very circus freak. It's why I wear the thick-framed glasses —to offset the shock.

"Yes, that's me; Lucy." I offer the polite smile I practiced on the drive over. "It's a pleasure to meet you."

We shake hands, his large and calloused. "It's so nice to finally meet you. I'm Thomas."

Yes, I know who you are. Thomas Caine, the high-school political science teacher turned famous bladesmith—otherwise known as my new boss. And he's even more handsome than in his Google images.

I tuck a strand of hair behind my ear, feeling the sting of insecurity. I wonder what Thomas thinks of an almost-forty-year-old woman applying for a nanny position. I should be running my own company, not running out of gas.

I'm surprised by how nervous I am.

"Come in," he says, gesturing at the downpour. "I'm thrilled you're here."

The first thing I notice is the smell of the home—rich leather and vanilla-scented candles. *Real* vanilla, not the nause-atingly sweet imitation stuff.

As Mr. Caine shuts the door behind me, I have to force myself not to gawk at the interior of the home. Windows are *everywhere* and even through the bleak, gloomy weather it's like living within a kaleidoscope. The natural light floods in from every direction, creating shadows across the modern aesthetic of the home.

"You have a—a beautiful home," I stutter. Why am I so damn nervous?

"Thank you. It's a bit secluded..." His voice trails off, and I get the sense he's insecure about this. He nods at my empty hands. "No bag?"

"They're in the car." (Along with everything else I own.)

"We'll get them later. I was thinking we could start by having a cup of coffee together. Do you drink coffee?"

"I do."

"Good. I couldn't survive without it. We'll get a cup and discuss your role in greater detail. Then I'll show you to your room. Soon, Consuelo, the housekeeper will be here—you'll love her. She'll show you around the property and the rest of the home. I'd do it, but I'm on a tight deadline."

I didn't realize knife-makers had deadlines.

I follow Mr. Caine through a great room with one of the

biggest fireplaces I've ever seen. But, like everything else, it's super modern. Gleaming slate gray with sharp corners. Black and white monochrome furniture complete the space.

"Consuelo is usually here only Mondays, Wednesdays, and Fridays," Mr. Caine says, "but she's going to come every day for a while to make sure you get acclimated."

We step into a wide hallway with wood paneling and marble floors. A collection of framed photos line the walls, featuring Mr. Caine gifting a political figure one of his exclusive engraved knives. The last one, the largest, is of him and the First Lady. Engraved on a framed sword is a famous quote from Eleanor Roosevelt. Surrounding the quote is a detailed nature scene, every minute detail perfect. This is what Thomas is known for, engraving monumental moments in political history on blades with a meticulous eye for detail. His work has been showcased in exhibits all over the country. Rumor is, he's made a boatload of money selling his art. Apparently the rumor is true.

I can't help but wonder why I was hired. I feel like a fish out of water here.

Mr. Caine offers a crooked smile. "Sorry, this is my ego wall. It's obnoxious, I know."

"It's impressive." But also odd is that there's not a single picture of the wife I'm here to babysit. Or children, for that matter. In fact I haven't seen a single thing to indicate that Mr. Caine has a wife. Not even a ring on his finger.

"Thanks," he says. "My job is why I live in the middle of nowhere. No distractions; no one ever stops by. I can work all day in my shop, uninterrupted." He shrugs.

It hits me then that perhaps this is why *I* was hired. Why Mr. Caine resorted to help-wanted ads instead of utilizing one of the many in-home care companies in the area. Who, in their right mind, would accept a live-in job in such a remote area?

Only someone at the end of their rope.

Like me.

TWO
EMILIA

Then

The moment I first laid eyes on Thomas Caine I knew he was the one. Fireworks, but without the kiss. It was an instinct. A deep-down gut feeling. Like the sun, moon, and stars suddenly aligned and, for one split second, the world was in perfect harmony. I know this sounds very *Jane Eyre*, but it's true; it's exactly how I felt.

I was twenty-three, waitressing at a coffee shop while failing out of law school. Smart enough to get in, not smart enough to want to stay. I was in that weird early-twenties stage where society expects us to automatically become productive citizens, but in reality, I was still eating Fruit Loops for dinner.

Then I met Thomas.

He was sitting in the back of the coffee shop, under a flickering light that made the corner appear like its own little night club. My regulars avoided the table for that very reason.

I didn't realize how handsome he was at first, because I was too curious how anyone could sit under such an obnoxious flickering light. But he was so engrossed in whatever he was doing, nothing else mattered.

Then he looked up and our eyes met.

Instant butterflies. Stars, moon, and all that.

He wore a tweed jacket, tortoiseshell glasses, and had a head of thick brown hair, sticking up as if he'd just run his hands through it. A cool, hipster vibe. I could easily imagine him winding down at night with a cigarillo in one hand, and a steamed mushroom latte in the other. Super cool, and *super* dreamy.

Balancing a tray of empty mugs, I sauntered over to him. My white-blonde hair—the only feature that saved me from looking like a teenage boy—caught the flickering light. At least I'd worn makeup and my padded bra that day. Small victories.

"Hi," I smiled, cocking a hip on the edge of the table. It teetered under my weight, but by God's grace, the tray remained balanced on the palm of my hand. Crisis averted.

He eyed me with interest, a smirk curling on generous lips. God, he had good lips.

"I like your hair," he said.

"I like your earring."

"It's a mole."

"Welp..." I stood. "I'll see myself out."

"Wait!" He chuckled. "Stop. I'm joking."

Grinning, I turned back. Witty banter officially ignited.

"Well, it *is* a mole," he confirmed, "but I'm not offended that you thought it was an earring. In fact, you're not the first to think so."

I frowned at the opened sketch book on the table. "Are you drawing a penis?"

His laughter was so loud that people looked over. My insides lit up.

"Yep," he mocked, wiping the tears from his eyes, "I'm drawing a self-portrait."

"Impressive."

"No, it's not a penis, you pervert." He winked. "It's an artillery cannon, actually. The beginning of one. The outline."

Of all the things I expected him to be drawing, that was not one of them.

"I'm sketching a scene from the Revolutionary War."

"You like to sketch bloody war scenes?"

"I do. Is it my turn to see myself out?"

"I see your weird obsession with large pieces of artillery—" I winked this time (this earning me another laugh) "—and I raise you an obsession with talking about politics. I majored in political science."

His eyes widened. "No way—me too."

"No way."

"Way. I thought you looked familiar. We had a political science class together. You sat in the front; I sat in the back." He winked. "But I also think we might have had another class together, too. Do you take any teaching classes? I'm getting my teaching degree. I'm planning on teaching high school or college, not sure yet."

"Nope. No teaching classes."

"Theater." He squinted "Was it theater?"

Heat bloomed on my cheeks and I considered lying because: what a cliche. A struggling actress who worked at a coffee shop. But that was ridiculous. Why should I care about what a stranger thought of me?

Because he's not a stranger. You are going to marry this man.

"Yes. I recently took up an acting class to fill my elective hours."

"You look like an actress."

I shrugged, sweeping a strand of hair away from my face.

"Anyway." He stood, thrust out his hand. "I'm Thomas Caine. A huge political science geek who loves to sketch bloody war scenes."

"I'm Emilia." Our hands clasped. "A political party fence straddler who believes in a woman's right to choose what she does with her body, but also in limited government and free markets."

"Marry me, Emilia."

"Right after you remove that mole, Thomas."

And that was it.

We married eight months—and one mole-removal surgery—later. Thomas's wedding gift to me was a self-portrait of the mole on his left ear, which hung above our kitchen table for years.

We moved into a studio apartment, ate ramen noodles (Fruit Loops when he'd allow it), and drank cheap wine. Watched trashy television, listened to old records, discussed politics for hours, and had sex every night. Eventually, Thomas got a job teaching at the local high school, while I worked as a legal assistant. Thomas was charming, funny, and smart. Those years were the happiest of my life.

Thomas drew me into a world of fantasy. One of love, friendship, incredible sex, old-school chivalry. I never wanted to leave him, never wanted to do anything without him. He was the remedy for my bad-decision habit that had plagued me for years.

How ironic that falling for him would prove to be the most dangerous decision of all.

THREE
LUCY

Now

Mr. Caine leads me into the kitchen. Natural light pours in from every angle, pooling on slate gray floors. The kitchen is as stunning as the rest of the home with modern minimalist design and upscale appliances. Gleaming granite countertops. Glass cabinetry. Sharp angles, monochrome colors. Not a speck of dust or smear of food anywhere. Rain-streaked windows frame a covered patio overlooking the forest below.

Mr. Caine motions to a breakfast nook in the corner. Beyond it is a dining room with a sixteen-chair dining table. I don't even know sixteen people.

"Have a seat, Lucy."

I settle into the black leather seat. Across the room, Mr. Caine operates a coffee pot that resembles a robot. I study him as he fills the water reservoir, dumps the grounds, warms the mugs in the sink. The quick, fluid movements of someone who has done it a million times. He appears to be rushed. To Mr. Caine, busy equals important. Type A, high anxiety. Most successful people are.

A few minutes later, I am sitting across from Thomas Caine in his five-thousand-square-foot glass house in northern Georgia. It is one of those pinch-yourself moments. For the last four months, I've been sleeping in the back of my Tahoe, showering at truck stops and eating garbage. Now, here I am.

I can't blow it.

Mr. Caine settles in, wrapping his hands around his coffee. The mug depicts a middle-fingered Clint Eastwood. So my boss has a sense of humor. Interesting. In my experience, I have found artists to be self-indulgent introverts who are incapable of small talk or witty banter.

"Firstly," he tilts his head, studying me with unsettling intensely, "I would love to know more about your business in California."

I'm prepared for this question. "Well..." I sip, swallow, set down the cup. "I am—was—a psychic."

Mr. Caine slaps the table with a boisterous laugh. "A *psychic!* Forgive me, but I'm *really* going to dive into this. I want to know everything. When did you learn you had the ability?" A wicked grin splits his impossibly handsome face. "Or is it all a ruse?"

"Well, you got me—I'm not a *true* psychic. I see auras. People's energy fields. In color."

"That's incredible. What does my aura say about me? Right now?"

"I can't see it."

"Oh no." He feigns horror. "I have no soul. I *knew* it."

I laugh despite myself. Mr. Caine is extremely charming. "The ability comes and goes. Sometimes I see them, sometimes I don't. I know it sounds wonky."

"No, it doesn't. I think it's fantastic. When did you learn you could do this?"

"Second grade."

I remember the exact day, time, and place, and what I was

wearing. I remember the smells, the lights, the sounds, every detail of that moment.

My teacher walked into the classroom and was glowing—literally encased in an orb of light. To say it unnerved me is an understatement. I was terrified. I kept looking around the room, but the other kids didn't appear to notice. That's when I realized only I could see it.

Then it started happening regularly, at random times, with random people—friends, my parents, the bus driver, the grocery store clerk. I couldn't control it. I thought I was sick, or worse, going crazy. This is a lot for an eight-year-old to process. It was an odd time—the beginning of, well, a very odd and unconventional life.

Eventually, I learned that this phenomenon is called synesthesia. (Yes, it's an actual medical diagnosis). In a nutshell, it's a very rare error in perception of senses. People with synesthesia experience one sense—touch, hearing, sight, smell, or taste—through another. They often see letters, or numbers, or sounds as colors. (Which leads to a slew of academic challenges, as you can imagine. I had terrible grades in school.)

"I didn't tell anyone for years."

"You had this incredible gift and didn't tell anyone?"

I cock my head. "You've been to junior high, right?"

Mr. Caine laughs. "I see. You would have been picked on, or worse, labeled a weirdo."

"Exactly. I didn't understand it, so how could I expect anyone else to?"

"I get it. And you make a living from this in LA?"

"I opened a shop called The Whispering Halo. It's a play on words. About how the aura, which can look like a halo, speaks to me. People would come to have their auras read, cleaned. Most were going through trauma or heartbreak." I don't mention that half the time I couldn't see anything at all. The older I got, the less my ability presented itself. Sometimes I worry it will leave me altogether. Then who am I?

"But now you're here..."

I nod. "Victim of the post-COVID economy. California was hit hard. People stopped spending money on frivolous things like aura readings. Eventually, I had to shut down the shop."

What I don't tell him is about the mounting debt, the eviction, the months of sleeping in my Tahoe, showering at truck stops, working odd jobs from town to town. About driving east because west would have taken me straight into the Pacific—which I considered, by the way.

Until now.

FOUR
EMILIA

Then

"I like other women."

I set down the wine I'd just poured and turned to face my husband of only one year. The sleet outside pinged against the kitchen window, a rhythmic patter that intensified the instant tension in the room.

Thomas stood in the kitchen doorway, backlit by the dim glow from the hallway. His face was flushed by the whiskey he'd been drinking all evening. His nerves were palpable, his eyes wild with anticipation of how I'd react.

For a long moment, neither of us spoke. I braced myself against the counter, fingers gripping the edge as my mind struggled to catch up to this abrupt confession.

I like other women.

"Okay," I responded slowly, carefully, drawing out the word to give myself time to process what was happening. "What do you mean, exactly?"

"I mean..." He shifted uncomfortably. "I'm attracted to other women."

I felt my stomach twist, but outwardly, I forced a calm demeanor.

"Are you cheating on me?"

"No!" Thomas said, crossing the room. "No, it's nothing like that—but I think I have a problem."

I stared at my husband, unblinking, my thoughts spinning too fast for me to grasp any single one. A *problem*. He called it a problem. The word hung between us, heavy, awkward. But I wasn't surprised, not entirely. Thomas had been acting different for months. At times distant, at others overly attentive, obsessively concerned with my schedule, planning my every move. Our sex life had slowed, too. I had noticed the change but assumed it was part of the adjustment to married life. Everyone says marriage changes people. I just hadn't expected this kind of change.

I didn't respond right away, filtering through the questions in my head: Should I be grateful that my husband had come to me with this? That he had the decency to confess instead of acting on whatever impulses he was having? Wasn't that what marriage was supposed to be—honesty, communication, working through problems together? Was this where I was supposed to grab his hand, and tell him everything was going to be okay?

But instead of gratitude, all I felt was a low simmer of anger.

Thomas exhaled a shaky breath, dragging his fingers through his hair. He started pacing. "It's always been like this," he said, "I just never told you. I've always had feelings for other women, but I thought it would go away. I thought once we got married, it would stop. But it hasn't. It's getting worse. The longer we're married, the worse it gets."

The *longer* we're married?

I closed my eyes in a feeble attempt to keep my anger in check. "Let me get this straight. You're telling me you have feelings for other women, and that's why you're here, confessing this to me?"

"Yes," he said, his voice firmer now, confident. "And the women always seem interested in me too—it's getting harder not to act on it."

And there it was—his ego. The ugly little (big) thing that had driven so many of our conversations. I realized early in our marriage that Thomas's inflated sense of self-importance went beyond what was considered normal. I diagnosed him with narcissism within the first six months of our courtship. I had even found it attractive at first. His confidence, his control—it had been a welcome contrast to the chaos of my own life. I liked how Thomas took charge, how he made me feel taken care of, even if that care bordered on control. Honestly? I found it kind of sexy. But now, that same ego was beginning to feel insidious, like something that threatened to unravel everything.

"But you're not cheating on me?" I asked again, needing to hear him say it one more time.

He shook his head.

"Thomas, I've got to be honest with you, I don't know how you're expecting me to respond here."

"I don't know either." He blew out a long breath, but this one was very different from the one a moment ago. This was one of relief. By listening to his confession, I'd unburdened my husband.

Well, you are freaking welcome, dear husband.

Anger boiled over and I felt that spark of attitude, the one I got before I made very bad decisions.

I crossed my arms over my chest. "Is it because you're unhappy in our marriage?"

"Don't do that, Emilia."

"Do what, exactly?"

"Manipulate the situation. Can't you just listen for once?"

"Fine. Let's get back to the point. So, you see a woman and get a crush on her. Is that right?"

"Yes. That's right." He was getting annoyed by that point, but found the fortitude to push through. "Even women I don't know, like a stranger at the grocery store. And then I'll fantasize about her for days."

"While having sex with me?"

He looked down—so that was a yes. Again, I wondered: why *the hell* is he telling me this?

"So... are you saying you want, like, a break, or something? A separation?"

"No. I just need your help."

"Okay. What kind of help are you asking for, exactly?"

"Help me want you..." His voice softened. "And *only* you." He stepped closer, cupping my cheeks like he used to in the beginning, back when everything was simpler.

"How?" I whispered, my mind racing with too many emotions to name—confusion, hurt, anger.

"By making me want you again," he said, his lips curving into a small, familiar smile. "*Only* you."

The manipulation was right there, obvious as a neon sign. He was turning his confession into something *I* needed to fix. Making his weakness my responsibility. And despite knowing this—despite the voice screaming in my head to run—I did what I thought a "good wife" was supposed to do.

I lowered to my knees and sucked him off.

After, as I rinsed my mouth in the bathroom sink, I caught my reflection in the mirror. I barely recognized the woman staring back at me.

FIVE

LUCY

Now

Once the coffee is finished, Mr. Caine asks if I'm ready to meet "her." *Her*, as in Emilia, the woman I will be taking care of. Yes, I say, despite the nerves churning in my stomach.

Thunder bellows overhead as I follow him to a floating steel staircase with sharp-edged handrails. Everything in this house is sharp, but perhaps I shouldn't be surprised considering the owner works with blades for a living.

"So," Mr. Caine says as we ascend the stairs, "you know from our interviews that my wife suffered a stroke a couple of years ago. She hasn't been the same since. One of the biggest challenges is that she lost her mobility and her ability to speak. She gets lots of headaches, too. Over the years her muscles have deteriorated, which has led to muscle atrophy. So, between the weakness and the headaches, unfortunately, Emilia is restricted to the master bedroom."

I hadn't realized how much assistance Mrs. Caine was going to require, and therefore, how challenging my job was going to be.

"Can she walk at all?" I ask.

"Yes, barely, and only with support and supervision. She rarely tries to anymore. I have to force her up."

He speaks very matter-of-factly. It comes off as cold and dispassionate, but then I remember that Mr. Caine has been a caregiver for years. At some point, I imagine the emotion subsides and life *must* go on. Which, I suspect, is exactly why he's hired me.

As if reading my thoughts, he says, "I have been Emilia's primary caregiver since the stroke. Consuelo, the housekeeper, helped tremendously in the beginning. But she couldn't keep up with the demand of both taking care of Emilia and cleaning the house, as you can imagine."

We reach the top of the staircase. The rain hammers the roof. A steady, drumming cadence that fills the silence. Much louder than the first floor. I notice the air is cooler than the rest of the house, and it's darker too, as if the light can't penetrate the ominous atmosphere of this floor. A dim hallway stretches out before us, lined with closed doors that seem to guard whatever lies beyond them.

"After Consuelo confessed that she couldn't take care of both the house and Emilia, I realized it was time to hire more help. You see, I have an exhibition coming up, and they have hard delivery dates that I cannot miss." He glances down but quickly recorrects.

Guilt. The man is riddled with it.

"Well..." I open my arms. "I'm here to help."

"Yes, and thank you. Okay." He claps his hands together, mood shifting back to casual. "In a nutshell, your job is to sit with her. To talk to her, to read her books. This is something I did a lot in the beginning, and we've noticed that her blood pressure lowers when she's being read to. You are in charge of feeding her as well. She can feed herself, but because of the muscle weakness, it's messy. Trust me, it's easier if you do it.

Emilia is very clumsy. You'll feed her multiple times a day—don't worry, I've got a schedule printed out—and also help dress and bathe her..."

My heart skips a beat. *Bathe?*

"...and lastly, be her friend. The doctor says it's possible that one day she'll be able to speak again. She might be more inclined to try if she has a friend around her all the time."

Mr. Caine peers longingly at the closed double-doors at the end of the hall. After a beat, his focus sharpens on me.

"As we discussed on the phone, you will be working twenty-four hours a day. You are to be at my wife's beck and call. This isn't a traditional eight-to-five job. She has a baby monitor in her room that will go off when there is significant movement. Anytime you're not with her, you are expected to have the monitor with you."

"I understand."

"I will pay you weekly, on Friday of each week, and as discussed, you live here rent-free, and eat for free. Use the gym, the pool, whatever you want. Consuelo gets the groceries, so you can tell her what you like, what you don't, or if you have any dietary restrictions."

"I'm not picky."

"I sleep in a room downstairs next to my shop. I often work until early in the morning and then crash. So, if you hear movement downstairs in the middle of the night, it's me, don't worry."

It strikes me as odd that Mr. Caine sleeps so far away from his ailing wife.

"Oh, I will come in multiple times a day to administer Emilia's medicine. Other than that, you're expected to handle everything else. Are you ready to see your room?"

I nod. We fall into step together, my gaze locked on the doors at the end of the hall, but Mr. Caine peels away and steps into the room before it.

"This will be your room."

It's smaller than I imagined—considering the size of the house—and recently renovated. Built-in shelves bookend a bay window with padded seating. The room is painted light yellow, and I get the vibe that it was once intended to be a nursery, which would make sense considering it's adjacent to the master bedroom. I want to ask, but I don't. It feels too personal.

The room is furnished simply but comfortably. A bed, a dresser, a walk-in closet, and a large bathroom with a soaking tub. Definitely better than the Tahoe.

"It's okay?" Mr. Caine asks.

"Of course."

"Good. Consuelo can help you with your bags later, if you need it."

He catches me studying the single framed photo in the room.

"That's Emilia and her mother." His expression softens as he lifts it from the dresser. "Emilia was eight in that picture."

"Are they stomping grapes?"

He smiles. "Yep. This was taken in Italy—that's where Emilia was born and spent most of her childhood. She moved to the States to be with her grandmother after her mom passed away. Her aunt owned a small winery there and Emilia and her mom would stomp grapes every Sunday. She loved it. She misses Italy. She used to visit a lot." He chuckles fondly. "When we were dating, it wasn't uncommon for me to wake up to a note that read: *left for Italy, be home later*. And Emilia would be gone for a week." His face falls and he slides the photo back into place. Thunder rumbles overhead. "That was before, though. Anyway. Are you ready to meet her?"

No. "Yes."

"Follow me."

SIX
LUCY

Now

"Emilia?" Mr. Caine calls out, lightly knocking.

I make a mental note of the protocol: Always knock and call her name before entering the room.

Though there is no response from the other side, Mr. Caine turns the knob and opens the doors. The hinges squeak loudly.

A woman with snow-white hair is sitting in an armchair, her back to us, facing sweeping windows that overlook the mountains. A pale, veiny arm rests on the armrest. A long oval fingernail slowly scrapes the leather, dragging back and forth, back and forth.

Mr. Caine repeats her name as he crosses the bedroom.

I hesitate near the doorway, an uncomfortable sense of intrusion settling over me, as though I've stepped into a space I don't belong—a space meant only for her.

Massive metal beams crisscross the vaulted ceiling, adding a stark, industrial elegance to the room. Recessed lights cast a soft, ethereal glow that feels both enchanting and faintly unsettling in its dimness. A grand chandelier hangs from the center of the ceiling, dark and unused, its intricate design lost in shadow. Against the far wall, a king-size bed dominates the space, its perfectly arranged white and gray linens untouched. Across from the bed is a small seating area with two plush chairs, one of which Emilia occupies.

To the left, a pair of large frosted glass doors hint at a walk-in closet hidden beyond them, while another set of doors leads to what must be the master bathroom. The room feels expansive yet strangely closed off. It even smells different.

"You like watching the rain?" Mr. Caine asks his wife in a placating tone that reminds me of how a parent would address a toddler. It irritates me.

"It's beautiful, isn't it?" he asks her, referring to the view.

For a moment, we stare at the rivulets of rain snaking down the glass, at the gray, gloomy landscape behind it. It's quite depressing, if I'm being honest.

Mr. Caine summons me across the room. The nerves double as I hurry to meet my new charge. He shifts aside so that I can step in front of the chair.

Mrs. Caine is nothing like I expected. The woman is shockingly beautiful. A natural beauty, fit for the cover of *Vogue* magazine. Her skin is porcelain with barely any wrinkles for a woman of her age. A delicate, heart-shaped face is framed by a chin-length bob of beautiful white hair. The hair is so white that, for a split second, I think I'm seeing her aura—an ability I haven't had for some time now. The biggest surprise, however, is the pair of big blue eyes that find mine *instantly*.

"Hello. My name is Lucy."

"Lucy is going to stay with us for a while," Mr. Caine adds. "She's here to help with whatever you need."

If Emilia understands her husband, she doesn't show it. Her eyes are locked on mine.

"Lucy just got here. She'll be sleeping in the room next to yours. You two will be spending a lot of time together. Consuelo will still be here too, but she will be focusing primarily on the house and errands now."

I nod like I've been in on this plan from the beginning. Still, Emilia doesn't take her eyes off me.

Mr. Caine sends me a pitying glance, and I force a smile—*it's okay. I've got this.*

"Anyway..." He returns his focus to his wife. "I'm going to let your new friend settle in her room. But she'll be back soon."

A small rolling table sits next to Emilia. Mr. Caine taps a white device with a red button. "And you know if you need me, press this button."

The device is an emergency button, like a help-I've-fallen-and-I-can't-get-up alert. Mr. Caine must carry the matching one in his pocket.

"And that's the baby monitor," he tells me, gesturing to a white and yellow set next to the alert button. "Emilia doesn't have a cell phone, because she can't operate one. Also, I don't know if your phone has internet, but there's a laptop on the dresser that you can use anytime. Consuelo uses it sometimes."

"Great, thank you." This excites me because my cheap Walmart phone does not have internet capability. But of course I don't tell him that.

"Emilia likes to watch the birds," Mr. Caine says, noticing my interest in the pair of binoculars next to the monitor. "Oh, that reminds me, the house has a security system. I'll have Consuelo show you how to operate it and she'll give you the passcodes—she handles all of that stuff for me. Remember to disengage the alarm if you need to go outside in the middle of the night, or early in the morning."

I nod, barely hearing a word he's saying because I'm too busy gaping at the large collection of prescription pill bottles stacked on the rolling table. At least a dozen—maybe more. Most are sedatives.

I frown.

Why would a woman who had a stroke need so many different kinds of sedatives?

SEVEN
EMILIA

Then

The daily blow jobs began after Thomas made the request to "make me want you, and *only* you." It wasn't framed as a command, exactly, but the expectation hung in the air, heavy and unspoken—*daily*. I complied, because Thomas had a way of making his desires feel like my choices. Because saying no meant cold silences and subtle threats and the quiet fear that he'd find someone else who would say yes.

I began to feel detached, like I was watching myself from somewhere far away, wondering why I couldn't just say no. I felt guilty. I should want this. I should want him—I should want to *please* him. Instead, I found myself drifting farther away from the woman I once was, not realizing that it's not normal to change so much for another person. Newlywed or not.

Eventually, Thomas transformed back into the man I'd fallen in love with. The witty conversations returned, the deep discussions about politics and philosophy that had first drawn us together. He looked at me the way he used to in the coffee shop, like I was the most fascinating person he'd ever met. The wandering eye, the random crushes—gone. Erased, like they'd never happened.

And yet, while Thomas appeared satisfied, I remained haunted by the weight of his confession. Tortured by it. No matter how much effort I put into making him "want only me," I couldn't stop the gnawing thoughts and worries that my husband might someday cross the proverbial line into infidelity. I didn't understand why he would plant that seed in my mind, knowing it would grow into an obsession.

When Thomas left for work, went to the gym, or even ran simple errands, I couldn't stop wondering: *Is he falling in love with someone else right now? Or worse... is he meeting someone?*

The obsession took hold quickly. I started compiling a list of every woman he interacted with at his school—the teachers, the administrators, even the girls in his classrooms. I'd drive by their houses, note their license plates. When he would leave for the gym, I would leave shortly after, checking for his truck at each address on my list. My anxiety fed on every unknown, every imagined possibility, growing stronger with each unanswered question.

One night, fueled by too much wine and spiraling paranoia, I tried to hack into his email while he slept.

He caught me.

My heart nearly stopped when I heard his voice behind me, groggy but calm—almost as if he'd been expecting it. I braced myself for the explosion of anger. But instead, Thomas just stood there, quietly watching me with tired eyes. I apologized, groveled, cried. Begged for forgiveness.

"I get it," he said finally, looking down at where I had dropped to my knees on the floor. "If I were in your shoes, I'd probably do the same thing."

The words were perfect—exactly what I needed to hear. Too perfect. But I was so desperate for reassurance that I ignored the calculated edge in his voice, the way his eyes stayed cold even as he pulled me into his arms.

Later that night, after we made love, I cried; overwhelmed by what I thought was his kindness. I told myself everything would be okay, that we could work through this together.

But the anxiety never left. Even as our marriage outwardly thrived, the tension inside me only grew. I quit my book club, gave up my evening yoga class—anything that might take me away from Thomas in the evenings. I told myself it was to spend more time with him, but deep down, I knew it was fear. Fear that if I wasn't home, he might be thinking about someone else. Worse, he might be *with* someone else.

I threw myself into being the perfect wife. I cooked elaborate dinners every night, agonizing over each menu, trying to outdo myself with every meal. I wore only the clothes Thomas complimented me on, carefully curating my appearance based on what pleased him. My hair was always down—he liked it that way. Everything I did, every decision I made, revolved around keeping his attention fixed on me.

Looking back, it was a million little things that did me in. Little compromises made without thinking twice. Telling myself it was normal, that it's what love required. And by the time I noticed how far I'd fallen, how much I'd lost of myself, it was too late. I'd built a version of myself out of desperation— and now I was trapped. I didn't know how to go back to the old, carefree Emilia.

And then, as most slow-moving trainwrecks do, I hit rock bottom.

EIGHT
EMILIA

Then

It was Amy and Leslie's thirtieth birthday party. They were the wives of Thomas's old college roommates—women I barely knew. Thomas hated that I had friends but couldn't object since they were married to his buddies. When the invitation came, I accepted immediately—not because I longed for their company, but because I needed a taste of freedom from Thomas's control.

After kissing Thomas goodbye and promising to be home by ten o'clock, I stepped out of the house in a modest, knee-length dress he had approved of. The moment I drove out of view of the house, I pulled over and changed into a much shorter, tighter cocktail dress, paired with sky-high heels.

The act felt rebellious, almost illicit, like a teenager sneaking out of her room, defying the strict rules of my parents. For the first time in a long time, I felt like my old self—the version of me nobody could control or pin down. The one who didn't ask for permission or seek approval.

It felt good. For the first time in what felt like forever, I felt free. And it felt *right*.

I met the girls at a hole-in-the-wall club on the outskirts of town, overlooking a lake. Being the only dance hall in the area, The Blue Bronco drew in party-goers from the surrounding small towns—even smaller than ours.

The second I stepped over the sticky threshold, every head turned in my direction. And I *liked* it. The old me awakened. The fun, charismatic coffee shop waitress who could flirt her way into a hundred-dollar tip in under ten minutes. The woman who lived moment to moment, not worrying about being a perfect wife or choking on my husband's dick so that he wouldn't cheat on me.

Amy, Leslie, and I secured a back corner table and promptly ordered their specialty fishbowl with three straws—a literal fishbowl filled with neon-blue pure-grain alcohol.

Forty-five minutes later, we were plastered.

"That dude over by the pool tables cannot keep his eyes off you," Leslie slurred, jabbing an elbow into my ribs.

I followed their gaze to a tall, broad-shouldered man leaning casually against a pool table at the back of the room, a pool stick resting loosely in one hand. His dark hair was thick and tousled, as if he'd just run his fingers through it. Even in the dim lighting, I could see the sharp angles of his jawline and the way his full lips curved slightly into a seductive smirk. Leslie was right—he was definitely looking at me.

My stomach tickled with something that resembled butter-flies, an unfamiliar thrill I hadn't felt in a long time. He was strikingly handsome, effortlessly so, with that casual confidence younger men often have. The kind that makes them seem untouchable. And he *was* younger—much younger than me. Yet, despite that fact, or maybe because of it, I couldn't stop myself from holding his gaze a second longer than I should have.

Amy released a low alcohol-laced whistle. "Damn, he's hot. Who is he?"

"Not from here, or I'd know him," Leslie responded. "He's probably from Greenland or South Springs."

We watched as two young blondes approached him. Pool Guy greeted them, but kept his focus on me.

"Jesus," Amy whispered, taking in the heat between us. "He is undressing you with his eyes." Then, a snort. "Good thing Thomas isn't here."

At the mention of his name, I glanced at my wristwatch.

"Checking the time again?" Leslie scowled. "What is that, like, the twentieth time you've checked?"

Mildly embarrassed—and acutely aware that neither of their husbands had set curfew for them—I twisted my watch so that the face was hidden under my wrist. I looked back at Pool Guy, who was now encircled by a group of blondes. Irrationally irritated now, I took a long pull from the fishbowl.

Amy and Leslie were watching me.

"What?"

They glanced at each other in that way women do when they're hiding something.

"What?" I pressed.

"I don't know. I mean, does Thomas usually text you that much when you're not with him?"

I'm never not with him, I thought, but lied instead. "I think he's just worried about the crowd here. It's notoriously rowdy."

Another glance between the girls.

"What? What aren't you guys telling me?"

"It's just that," Leslie sucked in a breath, "we've heard some disturbing things about Thomas."

My stomach dropped. "*Disturbing?*"

"Yeah."

"Like what?"

"Like, he's *super* jealous. He got like, really possessive with one of his ex-girlfriends in college."

My pulse began to race. "Possessive how?"

"I don't know if it's true, but the rumor is that the girl, Jennifer, tried to break up with him and he didn't take it well. He began stalking her. Creepy stuff, like would stand outside her apartment in the middle of the night wearing all black."

"No way. You're lying."

Amy shrugged. "That's what she said. Apparently Thomas doesn't take rejection well. Or losing. Or any kind of failure. When she finally got the nerve to break up with him, he sent really terrible threatening emails to her."

"Thomas *threatened* her?"

"Yeah. In one email he told her he *owned* her. And like..." She looked again at Amy who was nodding feverishly. "There was some blackmail too. I guess he threatened to show naked pictures he took of her when they were together."

My cheeks burned from both shock and embarrassment.

"Well I don't know who she is but she's lying," I said, hating how defensive I sounded.

"There's something else, too," Leslie continued. By the tone, this revelation was going to be worse than the one before. "Ricky told me a few nights ago that he saw Thomas and Carla together, parked in the woods. You know that old park off Highway 14 that no one really goes to anymore? There. And she was in his truck..."

My body was so hot it felt like someone had poured battery acid over my skin. Ricky, who worked for the city Parks and Recreation Department, was Leslie's husband. Carla was Thomas's girlfriend before we met.

My brain was yelling at me to ask questions, to ask for verification. But my heart knew it was true.

The table fell silent and the sudden awkwardness between them and me became unbearable.

I looked down at my phone vibrating as Amy and Leslie changed the subject in a feeble attempt to clear the mood. The longer I sat there, the madder I became. At them, at him. At myself, too, for ignoring the little red flags for far too long.

Because in my gut, I believed every word of their story.

After slurping up the last dregs of the fishbowl, I excused myself from the table, having no clue where I was going. I didn't want to be with "my friends" anymore but I also didn't want to go home to the man who I was now certain was cheating on me. I was caught between two places I didn't belong, floating in this uncomfortable space. I felt hurt and embarrassed, but at the same time, I was desperate *not* to feel those emotions. It was an erratic, maddening sensation, like an itch beneath my skin that I couldn't reach. I wanted to jump out of my body, to escape myself entirely, if only for a little while.

I needed something to ground me, something to remind me that I wasn't unraveling completely. That I hadn't lost myself. That I was still *that woman*—the one who was carefree, funny, *fun*. The one who knew exactly who she was. But even as that thought passed through my mind, I felt a bitter laugh rise in my throat. Who was I kidding? I needed *someone else* to remind me. I needed affirmation that Thomas didn't *own me*.

I found that affirmation while bent over the toilet in the handicapped stall, having sex with Pool Guy.

NINE
LUCY

Now

After introducing me to Emilia, Thomas leaves me to settle into my new room. I retrieve my bags from the Tahoe and unpack. Spend time decompressing and acclimating myself to my new space. My new home.

By noon, I'm painfully bored, and ready to check out my new digs. Consuelo, the housekeeper, has yet to arrive for her afternoon shift so I decide to explore the Caine estate on my own.

I make a quick stop by Emilia's room and confirm she is still asleep on her bed, where Thomas placed her after our introduction. She naps a lot, he told me, and I'd be lying if I said this didn't please me. It's easier to take care of someone who sleeps most of the time, and that's just a fact.

The second floor is larger than I'd anticipated. The hallway opens to a gallery, which leads to another hallway with more rooms. Very maze-like.

The gallery features a dozen of Thomas's artisanal knives, each framed. I spend twenty minutes moving from knife to knife. Intricately engraved on each blade are battle scenes or depictions of monumental moments in history. Definitely not my thing. One, however, stands out from the rest. It's a sketch of an ear. Literally—a human ear with a large brown mole on the lobe. The scribbled script at the bottom reads:

Dedicated to my darling wife, Emilia, who holds everything together while I live vicariously in the past.

Firstly, I wonder why Mr. Caine would gift his wife an engraved image of an ear lobe. It must be some sort of inside joke. Then, I wonder what exactly Emilia was holding together. I want to know more about her, what she did before the stroke, and what led up to it.

In the corner of the gallery is a cabinet with a mishmash of books. I choose a modern-day retelling of *Rapunzel* to read to Emilia later. Book in hand, I venture into the hallway where I find an office (that appears unused), two more bedrooms and bathrooms, a media room, and finally, yet another bedroom.

Everything in this room is cloaked in blue—the walls, the bedspread, the curtains hanging limply, filtering the faint light that seeps through the window.

In the corner is a cluttered desk, overwhelmed with multiple computer monitors. Stacks of folders and papers cover the surface. A bulky printer perches atop a filing cabinet beside a well-worn gaming chair, its fabric fraying at the edges. It all looks normal at first glance, like any teenage boy's room—except it's not normal.

Not at all.

Hundreds of photos, newspaper clippings, articles, and hand-drawn maps are tacked up in a chaotic collage that stretches from wall to wall. Red yarn crisscrosses the clippings, connecting seemingly random points, turning the entire wall into a web of obsession. It looks like something out of a crime drama—like a detective's evidence board.

Something deep inside me screams *danger, danger, danger,* but I force myself to step further into the room, compelled by a mix of fear and curiosity. As I move closer to the pictures, a chill snakes up my spine. The photos are all of the same boy, spanning the years from infancy to high school. His big brown eyes and unruly head of white-blond hair make it clear—this is Emilia's son.

I study the boy's face in each photograph. There's a clear transformation in him over time. In the earliest photos, his smile is wide and joyful, his eyes gleaming with innocence and mischief. But as the years pass, something shifts. His eyes dim. The sparkle fades. In the most recent photo—taken sometime during his teenage years—his smile has withered into a mere ghost of what it once was, a dispassionate, hollow curve of his lips. But it's his eyes that haunt me most. They seem to cry out silently, filled with a pain that I can almost feel: sadness, confusion, inner turmoil. Torture.

Something cracks inside me—a sharp pang of empathy, grief for a boy whose suffering feels palpable.

I tear my gaze away from the photos and focus on the workstation. Stacks of folders and notebooks are piled haphazardly on the desk, interspersed with a clutter of articles, handwritten notes, and sticky notes covered in frantic scrawls.

4/10: Citgo gas station, possible sighting, someone called 911

4/10: Blue Accord spotted on 412, no lic plate

4/10: Blue Accord at Sunny's Park. Not his.

4/10: 3:30pm, Still have not received cell phone records. **FOLLOW UP****

*4/11: Blue accord spotted at Wal-Mart parking lot in Blue
Hope. Security cameras confirmed not his. (Change of lic plate?)*

There are at least two dozen of these notes, and some have arrows that connect to other notes.

Hand trembling, I pick up one of the articles.

Local Boy Missing

Local high school student James Caine, seventeen years old, was last seen on March 9, 2005. He was wearing dark denim jeans, black boots, and a black sweatshirt. According to his parents, James left for school and never came home. Rock Hill School staff reports that James never made it to school, and that his car was not photographed entering or leaving any of the school parking lots. Neither James nor his car has been seen since. Police are asking for your help in this investigation. If you have any information about the disappearance of James Caine, please call 555-423-3287...

TEN
EMILIA

Then

When I saw those two pink lines, my world stopped. The timing meant the baby could be Thomas's or Pool Guy's. I considered abortion—the "easiest" escape from this mess. But what if this was Thomas's child, the beginning of the family we'd once dreamed of? That thought alone kept me from tracking down Pool Guy. Why complicate things further when I wasn't even sure?

Next, I thought about keeping it all a secret. Pretend nothing had happened. Pretend I hadn't slept with a stranger in a honky-tonk bar. Pretend this baby was unquestionably Thomas's, and celebrate the fact that we were finally going to become a family. After all, it appeared that Thomas was keeping his own infidelity from me (though I had no proof). But that idea crumbled the moment I pictured the worst-case scenario: what if the baby didn't *look* like Thomas? What if it was glaringly obvious from the moment of birth that he wasn't the father? I couldn't risk that kind of fallout. The truth would eventually surface, whether I wanted it to or not.

For two agonizing weeks, I went back and forth, weighing every option, searching desperately for a way out of this nightmare. But in the end, I came to a single terrifying conclusion—I had to tell Thomas. There was no way around it. The guilt was eating me alive. No matter how much I dreaded it, I owed my husband the truth.

I chose a day that Thomas had a teacher in-service day at his school, without students present, and therefore would likely be less stressed. I wore the long, beige silk house dress Thomas had recently gifted me. It clung awkwardly to my frame, a reminder of how little room there was for the person I used to be in this marriage.

The moment I heard the grind of the garage door opening, my heart leapt into my throat. Unable to stand still, I paced back and forth across the kitchen, wringing my hands. When Thomas stepped inside, briefcase in hand, he looked exhausted. His once crisp dress shirt was wrinkled, and the khakis he'd left in that morning were creased and rumpled. His face was pale, eyes shadowed with fatigue, like he'd been fighting a losing battle all day.

For a split second, I considered backing out. I could wait, tell him another time—maybe tomorrow, maybe never. But it was too late. He'd already seen the look in my eyes.

"What's wrong?" Thomas frowned, dropping his briefcase onto the floor with a dull thud.

For a moment, I couldn't speak. My mouth went dry, my heart pounding so hard it echoed in my ears. The words were right there, hovering on the edge of my tongue, but I couldn't force them out.

Just say it!

"I'm pregnant, and I don't know if it's yours," I blurted, tears welling in my eyes. "The night I went to the dance club with the girls, I got really drunk, and I made a horrible decision with a stranger. I swear I haven't seen or spoken to him since. I'm so sorry, Thomas. I'm so, so sorry. I've packed a bag. If you want me to leave, I will—I understand, I deserve it—I'm so—"

"Leave me?" he interrupted, his sharp tone cutting through my rambling like a blade.

I stuttered, caught off guard by his reaction. Confused by his lack of outrage over the cheating itself. "Y-yes," I said hesitantly, "I assumed... you'd want me to leave."

"You're my *wife*."

The way he said it, as though it was a statement of absolute, irrefutable fact, sent a shiver down my spine. I opened my mouth to apologize again, but all that came out was a broken sob. I covered my face with my trembling hands, ashamed and humiliated.

For what felt like an eternity, Thomas didn't speak. He just stood there, watching me cry. In that moment, I felt one inch tall. And I felt like I deserved that.

Finally, he asked, "Did you tell anyone?"

I wiped the tears from my cheeks, struggling to compose myself. "No. I... I called Amy a few days later and got his name. His name is Eugene Holland. He lives in Greenland, about thirty minutes away."

"Why did you tell Amy you wanted his name?"

"I made up a story," I admitted, feeling so small under his sharp gaze. "I told her he followed me outside, and it freaked me out a bit. I just wanted to know who he was."

"And you didn't tell her that you had sex with him?"

"No. Of course not."

"Do not tell anyone. *Ever.* Do you understand me?"

I blinked, still thrown by his response. "Yes. I understand... so... are you saying..."

"Yes," he said with finality. "We will keep the baby."

My jaw dropped. Of all the reactions I had prepared for, this wasn't one of them. Relief flooded through me, overwhelming and unexpected. Before I could stop myself, I lunged forward, throwing my arms around his neck. "Thank you, thank you, Thomas. It could be yours. It probably is—"

"It *is* my baby," he said sharply in my ear.

"I think so, too," I lied, clinging to him desperately. "But if you'd feel better, we can get a paternity test..."

Thomas pulled back abruptly. "Absolutely not," he snapped, affronted. "Emilia, you are my wife. You are my everything. That baby is mine, just like you are mine. He or she will be raised as *my* child, and you will remain *mine*."

Mine—not ours.

"But... don't you want to know for sure?"

His eyes flashed, dark and possessive. "Do *you* want to know?"

Did I want to know?

"No," he answered for me. "The answer is no. I'll be damned if I'm going to share you—or this child—with another man. My baby or not."

It wasn't the words themselves that unsettled me—it was the intensity behind them. There was a finality in his tone, a dark edge that made my stomach twist with unease. Instinctively, I took a step back, and a draft of ice-cold air filled the space between us.

Thomas continued, his voice brisk and authoritative. "I don't want you hanging out with Amy and Leslie anymore."

"But they're my only friends."

"Friends?" he scoffed. "Your friends allowed you to put yourself in a dangerous situation with a stranger. That man could have killed you or kidnapped you. They're not good friends, Emilia. They're reckless and irresponsible. Give me their phone numbers."

Every instinct in me screamed to refuse, but my body moved on its own, driven by fear, by embarrassment, by shame. I walked to the kitchen junk drawer and retrieved the notebook where I kept contact information. My hands trembled as I handed it to him.

He slipped it into his pocket—*his* pocket.

"I'll call them tonight. They won't bother you again."

Bother me? "What will you tell them?"

"That you're going through something and need space." His tone was dismissive, as though that explained everything.

I blinked, processing. *Well, I am pregnant. Maybe it's for the best. Maybe it'll give me time to think without them pressuring me with invites...*

Thomas continued without missing a beat. "No more drinking. We'll throw out all the alcohol and stock up on clean, organic food for you. You'll need to quit work so you can rest. I'll sign us up for Parents-to-Be classes, first aid, and birthing courses. I'll call the insurance company tomorrow..."

No more friends.

No more work.

No more booze, processed foods.

I barely heard the rest. Thomas's words faded into the background as a strange sense of déjà vu washed over me. Memories of standing in this exact spot while Thomas told me about his attraction to other women flashed behind my eyes. And suddenly, a sick, twisted thought surfaced from the depths of my mind:

When Thomas told me he liked other women—had it all been a ruse? A calculated provocation, designed to test me, to push me into making a mistake? Or worse... had it been a form of manipulation, knowing that I would rebel in my own time. And when I did, he would have the upper hand in our marriage.

No. That's insane. No one—*no one*—is that manipulative.

ELEVEN
LUCY

Now

I clear my throat and glance at Emilia, curled in the armchair like a porcelain doll someone forgot to wind up. Her hands rest limp on the blanket draped over her lap, her gaze fixed somewhere beyond the window. I wonder what she sees out there—if she sees anything at all.

Opening the modern-day retelling of *Rapunzel*, I smooth my fingers over the pages and begin.

"In a city where towers stretch into the sky, there is a girl locked away. Her hair is not golden but dark as ink, and instead of a witch, it is the weight of the world that keeps her trapped."

I steal a glance at her. Nothing. So, I press on, letting the words wrap around us.

"The world moves on without her, people rushing past, never looking up. She wonders if she is real or if she is only a story whispered in the wind."

A flicker—just the smallest shift in her eyes. I hold my breath, unsure if I imagined it.

I lean forward, the book balanced on my knee.

"Then, one day, someone looks up. A boy, not a prince, but someone who sees her, really sees her."

Emilia's fingers twitch, barely perceptible.

I keep reading, my voice softer now, like I'm telling her a secret. *"And in that moment, for the first time in a long time, she wonders if she might still be real."*

I watch her, waiting. Hoping. However, I get nothing else.

As I continue the story, my mind keeps drifting to the missing boy. It's a nagging thought I can't shake, like a pebble lodged in my shoe. I want to ask her about it, to hear her version of what happened, but I know that would be wildly inappropriate. Besides, she can't speak—not in a way I can understand, anyway. She mumbles now and then, soft and unintelligible, but it never forms into anything coherent. Still, that doesn't stop my imagination from running wild. I can't help but wonder if grief is what broke Emilia. If her stroke was caused by a heart too shattered to keep going.

I glance up again. Emilia isn't staring past me anymore. She's watching *me*. Her eyes latch onto mine with startling clarity—and I swear I see moisture gathering at the edges.

Tears.

I swallow hard and reach for the tissue box on the side table. I pull one free and lean in, dabbing gently at the corners of her eyes. Her skin is warm beneath my touch, her lashes damp.

I press the tissue into her hand, curling her fingers around it. For a long moment, she just sits there. Then, so faint I almost don't notice, her grip tightens.

And that small squeeze feels like the loudest thing in the world.

We sit in silence for a long moment, before she closes her eyes—as if exhausted by the emotion—and rests her head against the chair.

I close the book. It's time for another nap, anyway. The first one was a mess. Or rather, moving her to the armchair after was a mess. It was like lifting a wet blanket from the clothes washer. I'm not nearly as strong as I used to be, and I found myself huffing, puffing, and nearly slipping several times as I tried to maneuver her into place. I imagine the scene would have looked comical to anyone watching, but for me, it was unsettling. The thought of Emilia being so helpless during a real emergency—a fire, a break-in, even a severe storm—left me deeply uneasy. And once again, I found myself questioning why her husband sleeps downstairs, so far away, on the opposite end of the house.

I feel terrible for her. This woman—once beautiful, vibrant, married to a renowned artist—lost her son, then her health, and finally her autonomy. It's the kind of tragedy that feels almost too cruel to be real, the kind of story that leaves you with only two choices: run away from the wreckage or stay and try to help pick up the pieces.

I want to help. How could I not?

I've just begun pulling back the sheets when the doorbell rings—the same damn *Stars and Stripes* tune as before. I glance at the clock—3:04 p.m.—then shift my gaze to Emilia in the armchair, staring out the window with a vacant expression.

I pause, unsure if answering the door is part of my responsibilities.

When the doorbell rings again, I decide to take initiative, mainly because I cannot bear to hear that damn song again.

"I'll be right back, Mrs. Caine." I slide the book on the rolling table. "Do you need anything while I'm downstairs?"

Although I know Emilia won't answer me, I give her the opportunity to try to speak. At the very least, I want her to know that I am not going to treat her like an imbecile, like her husband does.

When Emilia makes no acknowledgment that she heard me, I jog downstairs and open the door.

I'm momentarily taken aback by the woman standing on the

doorstep. She's striking—just as beautiful as Emilia, though in a completely different way. While Mrs. Caine exudes an air of timeless elegance with her willowy frame, perfectly cut blonde bob, and soft, delicate features, this woman carries herself with confident poise. Her long, jet-black hair whips gently in the wind. Her eyes glint with a kind of sharpness, a perceptiveness born of necessity. There's a certain guardedness in her stance, like someone who's learned to be watchful. A faded scar runs along her cheek.

In a nutshell, this woman is a badass. I'd place her somewhere in her mid-forties, slightly older than myself—yet I look *nothing* like that.

Thomas Caine must love beautiful women. I'm lucky our interviews were over the phone. I might not have gotten hired otherwise.

"You must be Lucy," she says. She doesn't linger on the freakshow that is my two different colored eyes. "I'm Consuelo, the housekeeper."

"Nice to meet you." I step back, open the door wide.

Consuelo hangs her purse in the coat closet next to the front door. "Has Thomas given you the full tour?"

Along with her cardigan and white T-shirt, she's wearing black slacks and ballet flats. Aside from the cardigan, we match exactly, and I mentally pat myself on the back for my good sense in choosing something that resembled a uniform.

"Not the full tour," I say. "Only the kitchen and a few rooms upstairs."

We cross the foyer. She walks quickly, with purpose, as if she's got a lot to do.

"Is he in his shop?" she asks, distracted.

"Yes, I think so."

"Good, I'm late. My brother called and I had to talk him off a cliff. Metaphorically. Anyway, Thomas is always in his shop. He's a workaholic. He'll work until three or four in the morning so don't be alarmed if you hear someone moving in the house late at night."

"He warned me."

"Did he? Good." Her gaze flickers down the hallway, then quickly over her shoulder.

I'm catching a strange vibe from Consuelo, though I can't quite put my psychic finger on it.

TWELVE
EMILIA

Then

When James was born, my entire world tilted on its axis. What had been a self-centered existence was replaced in an instant by a fierce, primal possessiveness. I hadn't known it was possible to feel so much at once: awe, love, fear. But from that moment on, my single, consuming goal in life was to protect my child.

I remember everything about that first moment—his tiny, wrinkled body pressed against my bare chest, the warmth of his skin. His soft, grayish complexion, sticky with afterbirth. The sweet, earthy scent of his hair, like the air before a summer storm. His impossibly small fingers, tipped with sharp, delicate nails that grazed my skin. I loved every part of him. Every perfect, tiny detail. It felt like something out of a fairytale, the kind of moment you're supposed to treasure forever. But there was one thing missing—one glaring absence in this picture-perfect moment.

Even in that euphoric haze of new motherhood, I knew immediately, with absolute certainty that James wasn't Thomas's child. And from the cold flicker in Thomas's eyes, I knew he knew it too. While James had inherited my snow-white hair, the rest of him was unfamiliar—his nose, his eyes, the curve of his lips. None of it belonged to Thomas. But I knew that his eyes—those chocolate-brown irises with little gold flecks—were just like the man I slept with in the bar. Pool Guy, aka, Eugene. Aka, James's birth father.

There was no more room for doubt. The truth hung between us like a shadow, unspoken but heavy. And despite Thomas's earlier proclamations that he would raise the baby as if he were his own, his disinterest in James was evident from the start.

When the nurse offered him the chance to hold our five-minute-old son, Thomas declined without hesitation. "I'll wait until they clean him up," he said, his voice distant, detached.

While the nurses stitched my torn cervix, they took James across the room to check his vitals. They asked Thomas if he wanted to help. I could sense his reluctance, but being the charming, charismatic man he is, Thomas put on the face of a doting father and stepped up to the plate. That's the thing about Thomas: He knows how to read (and work) a room. Women adore him. Men admire him. He was always the endearing husband, the charismatic friend. He stepped forward, going through the motions like an actor hitting his marks. But there was one moment—one slip—that no one else caught. The flash of raw fear in his expression when the nurses weren't looking.

I don't think it was fear of James, or even of the responsibility of being a father—it was the fear of losing control over the life he had meticulously built. Fear of how James's presence would ripple through everything he had worked so hard to maintain—his career, his marriage, his carefully curated routines, even his newfound obsession with bladesmithing.

Even through the fog of pain and medication, I felt a knot form in my stomach—a warning bell, faint but insistent. In that moment, I knew, without question, that somewhere, somehow, I had made a terrible, terrible mistake.

By the time James was two weeks old, he had been diagnosed with colic. The incessant, high-pitched cries filled our days and stretched our nights into endless marathons of exhaustion. I tried everything—cutting dairy from my diet, buying expensive anti-colic bottles, lavender oils, warm baths. Nothing worked. The doctors reassured me it would pass by twelve weeks, but that did nothing to ease the torment of those sleepless nights.

For me, anyway. By then, Thomas had checked out entirely. He distanced himself from us, retreating into his shop, leaving me to shoulder the burden alone. One morning, desperate and drained, I asked if he regretted his decision not to get a paternity test.

"I told you, Emilia. I will not share you with another man," he said, his voice cold and final, before walking down the hall and disappearing into the garage, where he practiced blade-smithing.

There was a moment—just a fleeting one—when I considered reaching out to Eugene. But then I remembered how young he was. He would be a child raising a child. I couldn't bring myself to contact him. I couldn't shatter his world with the news that he now had a child he never asked for. What good would it do? It wouldn't change anything. It wouldn't make Thomas care more. It would only make things messier.

By the fourth week of colic, I was running on fumes, teetering on the edge of collapse. One night, utterly spent, I marched into the garage, which Thomas had turned into a shop. He was hunched over his workbench, earbuds in, engrossed in whatever blade he was crafting. Without a word, I placed James on his lap, turned on my heel, and stormed out of the room. I crawled into bed, desperate for even a few minutes of sleep, but something wouldn't let me rest.

A mother's instinct, maybe. I don't know.

At one in the morning, unable to ignore the nagging feeling, I got out of bed and made my way down the hall. As I neared the garage, I heard James's muffled cries, faint but persistent, echoing through the cold air. I broke into a jog and shoved the door open.

There, on the cold concrete floor, lay James's tiny, four-week-old body. He was on his stomach, his fragile limbs flailing weakly, his neck twisted awkwardly to the side. His skin was bright red, flushed from the force of his screams, his little face contorted in distress.

Thomas stood over him, earbuds in, studying his struggling child. The look on his face this time, however, was not of dispassion, it was of disgust.

Clutched in his hand was a drill.

THIRTEEN
LUCY

Now

Consuelo and I step into the kitchen. She retrieves a clipboard from the pantry and scribbles a few notes. Her sign-in log, I assume. The sleeve of her cardigan slips up slightly, revealing a bevy of tattoos on her forearm. The centerpiece is a large cross. Inside are lines of birth dates. Five of them.

"Not my kids," she says, catching me looking. "I don't have any. They're for my brothers and sisters. All younger than me."

I gasp. "Oh my—I'm so sorry."

"No, it's not a tribute," she chuckles. "They're not dead. We're just very close. In heart, anyway. We all have matching tattoos."

"Do they live around here?"

"No." Her expression hardens. "They're back in Mexico, where I grew up." She tugs down her sleeve and replaces the clipboard. "I miss them. I worry about them."

Despite Consuelo's tough exterior, I sense a deep sadness. Layers of trauma covered under a tough-girl persona. I wish could see her aura. I'm certain it would be fifty shades of muddy.

"So," she says. "Want me to give you the tour now?"

"I'd love that, thanks. Am I supposed to sign the clipboard like you did?"

"No, since you live here you don't need to log your hours. Don't worry, I'll walk you through everything."

We fall into easy conversation as she takes me through the first floor. Like Thomas, Consuelo has many questions about my psychic ability. But I keep things short and simple because there are plenty of other things I'd like to talk about instead. Like what's the strange dynamic between Thomas and Emilia, and Consuelo's take on what happened to their son? But I need to tread lightly. I don't want to get fired for snooping in closed-door rooms.

In addition to the living area and kitchen, the first floor consists of a home gym, a wine cellar, an indoor pool, guest quarters, and a laundry room the size of the apartment I was evicted from in LA after my business failed. Thomas's shop is a standalone structure connected to the home by a glass breezeway. It resembles an industrial lodge with stone and timber accents and a sleek steel-reinforced entrance. We step outside, and I peek into one of the windows.

The workshop has an expansive, open floor plan with designated zones for forging, grinding, polishing, and assembly. Floors made of polished concrete. The ceilings are tall to accommodate the heat and smoke of the forge, equipped with an advanced ventilation system to ensure clean air and maintain a comfortable temperature. The space is illuminated by high-intensity LED lighting for precision work, supplemented by large windows and skylights for natural light. Walls of tools and equipment stretch the entire length of the building. I imagine this space cost nearly as much as the home.

Next to the breezeway is another guest bedroom. Next to that, a four-car garage.

"Woah." I gawk at the vintage Porsche in the last bay.

"I know," she says. "Nice, huh?"

"Uh, yeah."

"He let me drive it into town a few times. It was awesome. Oh, that reminds me. The nearest gas station is thirty minutes away. If you ever need gas, Thomas keeps cans in here. They're behind the four-wheelers."

"Thanks for the heads up." I slide her the side-eye. "You've had to use them, haven't you?"

She laughs and nods. "Twice. I'm terrible about keeping my car low on gas. Thomas had to save me from the side of the road once. Come on, I'll take you out back."

A multi-level patio stretches the entire length of the home, sprawling across most of the backyard in clean, precise lines. Beyond the patio, the land slopes sharply downward, offering an unobstructed view of distant mountains rising against the horizon. Though the storm has passed, the sky remains a dreary slate gray, its color perfectly matching the trim of the house. Low-hanging clouds cling to the mountain peaks, swirling around them like ghostly shrouds. Raindrops continue to fall from the trees and awnings, landing in heavy splats on the cold stone slabs.

"The place is amazing, isn't it?" Consuelo rests her hands on her hips and gazes at the trees. "Past that copse of trees is a cliff with killer views. Thomas made a special bench for Emilia there."

"I'll check it out. This is one of the nicest houses I've ever seen."

"Thomas has done very well for himself."

I note the mark of pride in her voice, and also that she refers to him as Thomas instead of Mr. Caine.

"When did they build it?" I ask.

"Four-ish years ago. *Before* Emilia's stroke, if that's what you're about to ask." Consuelo extends her finger, catching a raindrop on the tip. Her nails are long and red. "You want to know the funny thing? She's the one who chose this location. And she doesn't even get to enjoy it." She pauses. "Thomas didn't want to live all the way out here, but they made a deal. He allowed her to choose the location, if she'd let him design the house. They have completely different aesthetics. Thomas would have preferred to move to a city, so he built a city house. While Emilia would rather live in a log cabin."

"How long have you worked for the Caines?"

"A long time." Consuelo purses her lips. "Almost twenty years now."

So, you started about the same time their son went missing. Interesting.

"A lot has changed since then." She hesitates, then turns back to the house. "Anyway. Have you met Emilia?"

"Yes, when I got here."

Consuelo lingers as if she's waiting for my impression.

Honestly, I'm not sure what my first impression is. When I first met Emilia, she locked eyes with mine with an intensity that was unsettling. But after her nap, she seemed like a different person—entirely vacant, unresponsive, drooling. The contrast was jarring. Even more shocking was her husband's complete indifference to her condition.

"Well," Consuelo says, "if you have any questions about the process of caring for her, let me know." She pivots. "Let's head to the second floor."

Consuelo walks me through the library, the media room, and the additional bedrooms. She gestures to the last room, the one that I know contains the missing-boy wall. "And... that's the tour."

"Wait. Whose bedroom is that, at the end of the hall?"

"That's Emilia's room."

"Is it?" I frown. "I thought her room was the master bedroom."

"Well, it's not *her* room, technically, but Emilia considers it her room."

"What's in it?" I ask, though I already know.

Consuelo regards me, a small smile spreading across her red lips. "You might be the psychic between us, Miss Greer, but I am an expert reader of bullshit."

"I—I, uh..."

"You already went in there, didn't you?"

I exhale, dropping my head. "I did. I was bored and snooped. I'm sorry. Please don't tell Mr. Caine."

"I won't tell him, and I did it too, don't worry."

"Can we talk about it?"

She squints, contemplating the question, and for the first time, I see something other than strength and composure in the housekeeper's eyes.

FOURTEEN
EMILIA

Then

It was a regular Tuesday morning when I found the letter in the mail. The return address stopped me cold. The letter was from Eugene, James's birth father. He had found me. His words were unexpected—he'd never stopped thinking about me. Hope flared, ridiculous and fleeting. Could this be my chance? Maybe Eugene wanted a family? Maybe he could be my way out. I debated telling him the truth, but in the end, I couldn't lie. My response was awkward and blunt—*Funny story, I got pregnant that night. Pretty sure he's yours.*

To no one's surprise, Eugene didn't take it well. He demanded a paternity test. I couldn't blame him. So one morning, after Thomas left for work, I packed James into the car and drove to Eugene's hometown.

The moment Eugene saw James, he went pale. The resemblance was undeniable. Then, he looked at me like I had ruined his life. When the results confirmed what we both already knew, he didn't offer apologies—just a lawyer. That was when I knew I couldn't hide this from Thomas any longer.

Telling him was worse than I imagined. In the kitchen, he listened in stone-cold silence before unleashing his fury. He called me an ungrateful, deceitful bitch. Reminded me that he paid for everything—for me, for James. And now, because of me, he'd have to pay legal fees too. He demanded the letters, which included Eugene's telephone number, taking away my right to speak to Eugene at all.

"No one will ever love you like I do," he said. "No one else would stay with you and raise a child that isn't his. You should be grateful", he told me. "You're lucky I'm here."

I held James close, silent. Because deep down, a part of me believed him.

Months later, Eugene and Thomas met at a quiet park on the outskirts of town. I was told to wait in the car. The command wasn't explicit—it never was with Thomas—but we both knew what would happen if I disobeyed.

I watched, helpless, as Thomas carried James toward my one-night stand, playing the role of doting father. His smile was easy, his steps confident, as if this was just another piece of his perfectly controlled world. I gripped the steering wheel until my knuckles went white.

After that, once a month, Thomas brought James to the park for visitation. And once a month, I sat in that same car, feeling invisible. Outside of these carefully scheduled visits, Thomas barely acknowledged James. But when it was time to play the role of Dad, he transformed, adopting the part with all the pride and vigor expected of a hero.

Meanwhile, I began to disappear. I'd already quit my job. I cut my hair. Stopped wearing makeup. Began dressing in shape-less baggy clothing. I convinced myself that this was my life now, and that I should be grateful. That Thomas was a hero for accepting James, for putting a roof over my baby's head, for paying for the food, medical bills. And I was grateful—I really was.

I was also completely brainwashed.

I'd convinced myself that the only thing that mattered was James—that Thomas provided stability, and my son deserved that, even if I had to lose myself in the process.

Days blurred into weeks, then into years. Thomas's blade-smithing hobby took off and his career soared, bringing wealth, recognition, and the envy of everyone in town. Invitations to dinners and parties poured in, and with each event, I perfected the art of masking my reality. To the outside world, I was the happy homemaker, the supportive wife of a successful man. But inside, I was hollow, living a double life: one where I smiled for appearances, and another where I barely recognized the woman in the mirror.

It took me many, *many* years to understand that the manipulation that Thomas put me through was abuse. But I didn't call it that at first. I convinced myself it wasn't real because there were no bruises. *At least it's not physical,* I told myself again and again, as if that made it any less damaging.

How wrong I was.

All forms of abuse leave scars. And most often, it's the ones you can't see that hurt the most.

FIFTEEN
LUCY

Now

Like an eager teenager in a circle of gossip, I'm on pins and needles when I realize Consuelo is going to divulge the details surrounding Emilia and Thomas's missing son.

We're back in the kitchen now, preparing Thomas's afternoon snack. The room is warm, filled with the comforting scent of brewing coffee and the soft chop of a knife against a cutting board. Consuelo is slicing strawberries while I arrange cubes of cheese on a charcuterie board. The marble countertop is covered in containers of fresh fruit, prosciutto, nuts, and crackers.

"So," I prompt, stealing a grape from the pile. "James."

Consuelo lets out a long breath. "Yes. Thomas and Emilia had a son."

Had.

She pops a strawberry in her mouth, chews, swallows. "He went missing about a year before I was hired. In fact, it's why I was hired. To help clean the house while things fell apart. James was seventeen years old. He left for school one morning and never came back. Didn't you Google Thomas Caine before you accepted the job?"

"I did, but I didn't see anything about a missing son."

"It's been a long time. Old news, I guess."

"They haven't seen or heard from him in twenty years?"

Consuelo shakes her head as she arranges the strawberries on the board, fanning them out with ease and precision. I wonder how many of these boards she's made.

"Grapes, there." She taps the board with her pinky. "The case went cold," she continues. "In fact, I think the state officially considers James to be deceased at this point. They might even have a death certificate for him. But who knows, it's as if James disappeared into thin air. It's a horrible, horrible thing. Every parent's nightmare. Well, Emilia's anyway."

"What do you mean, Emilia's anyway?"

"James is not Thomas's."

"What?" I squeak.

"*Shh!*" Consuelo puts her finger to lips, glancing over her shoulder, then returns her focus to the board. "The rumor is Emilia met a guy at a bar one night and got pregnant. This was *after* she and Thomas married."

"And they stayed together, despite that?"

Consuelo nods, then pauses, as if considering her next words carefully. "Thomas doesn't like to let things go."

"What do you mean?"

"He's possessive. Once he sets his sights on something, he gets it, and he keeps it. Just like he set his sights on becoming successful." She gestures around the house. "And look at him now. Anyway, when James went missing it was hard for everybody. While Thomas coped by getting lost in his work, Emilia obsessed over it."

I recall the dedication Thomas wrote in one of his paintings:

Dedicated to my darling wife, Emilia, who holds everything together while I live vicariously in the past.

Next, Consuelo slices a ripe pear into delicate, crescent-shaped slivers, placing them in a neat fan beside a pile of glossy red grapes. "After James went missing, Emilia ran her own rogue investigation. She turned James's bedroom into a control center. She called it her 'office.' She would spend every day in there. Thomas tried to get her help—therapy, a psychiatrist, the works—but she denied it. They had a lot of problems to begin with, but this exacerbated it. In fact, Emilia had served him divorce papers right before James went missing."

"Why?" I begin sorting the cashews and almonds.

"I don't know. I do know Emilia served again, years later. But neither would sign, despite basically hating one another. It's like they knew they were the only people who understood each other because of what they'd gone through. The whole thing is sad. Anyway, the room?" She jerks her chin upstairs. "It's an exact replica of James's room in the old house when he left that morning and never came back. She had it built and decorated to match exactly. The blue shirt that's lying on the bedspread? Did you see it?"

I nod.

"That shirt was on his bed when he left. It's in the exact location where he left it."

"Wow." I shake my head, then lift the small dish of honey-roasted almonds. "More nuts?"

Consuelo nods, drizzling a thin stream of honey over a wheel of camembert before tucking in a sprig of rosemary for a final touch.

"And you've been working for them since then?" I ask, meticulously arranging the almonds.

Consuelo nods. "They lived about an hour southwest of here in a small town called Rock Hill. After everything happened, Thomas called the housekeeping service where I worked, and that's how we met. After they built this house and moved here, Thomas offered me good money to move closer and continue cleaning for him. I live with my boyfriend in a little rental about twenty minutes away. Sometimes I stay overnight here if there is extra work to be done."

My wheels begin to turn. It's hard to imagine Mr. Caine not being attracted to Consuelo. Especially while his wife is incapacitated.

Before I can tactfully ask if she and Mr. Caine are having an affair (is there a tactful way to do that?), she says, "We don't speak about James anymore."

"Yeah, I noticed there aren't even any pictures of him downstairs."

Consuelo solemnly nods. "I don't even know the last time Thomas said his name. It's how he deals—he doesn't."

"Do they think he ran away or was kidnapped?"

"Both angles were looked into extensively." Consuelo steps back to admire our work. The board is a full mix of textures and flavors—sweet, salty, creamy, and crisp. She nods, satisfied, then wipes her fingers on a towel and moves to the coffee. "At the end of the day," she continues, "there was no solid evidence to determine either way. James's cell phone was turned off and dismantled not long after he left the house that morning. It hasn't been turned on since, and they never found it. His car was also never found. Everyone—the entire town, it seemed— was interviewed. Everyone at school. There were massive search parties. Emilia was arrested twice for stalking people she wrongfully thought were involved."

"Arrested?"

"Yes."

"Wow." I shake my head. "What was Emilia's job during all of this? What did she do for work?"

"She had recently picked back up the legal assistant job she had before she got pregnant, but then quit again when James went missing. And then Thomas started making big money and she never went back to work... then the stroke. "

My heart cracks a little deeper.

"So there is no trace of their son, at all? No substantial evidence?"

Consuelo pours steaming coffee into a mug and sets the board and coffee on a tray. "The only thing that James always carried with him was a very expensive compass that Thomas once gifted him. Solid 24-carat gold and engraved with his name. Thomas has a matching one with his name. It was the only thing, aside from his backpack, that was not in the house after he went missing. The cops called every pawn shop in the entire state. I think Emilia even called the ones in the surrounding states—I'm not joking. She was hung up on that. She was certain he'd pawn it for money if he ran away. Or if he'd been kidnapped, the people who took him would. But it's never turned up anywhere." Consuelo glances at her watch, obviously wanting to move on from the subject. "I need to take this to Thomas and get started on my duties, and you need to get back to Emilia." She lifts the tray, indicating she's done with this conversation.

But I'm not.

"Wait. So, what caused Emilia's stroke many years later?"

"Stress, I guess. Prolonged stress does horrible things to the body. I need to get this to Thomas."

Before I can stop myself, I blurt, "Why doesn't Thomas take care of her? It seems like he doesn't want anything to do with her."

Consuelo turns, surprised by the audacity. He is my new boss, after all.

Her eyes narrow. "Thomas might have his issues, but he's just trying to make it through this world like everyone else." She pauses. May I give you a piece of advice?"

"Please."

"Emilia is your job. She is to have your undivided attention, *at all times*, do you understand?"

I nod.

"Emilia *only*."

With that, Consuelo steps past me and disappears down the hallway.

I don't need to ask what she meant. Her message was clear. *Stay away from Mr. Caine.*

SIXTEEN
EMILIA

Then

As Thomas's career soared, so did his mood. His aggressive, overbearing demeanor seemed to lessen under the glow of money and fame. He became lighter, freer, reveling in the validation of his success. For the first time in years, Thomas appeared genuinely proud—not just of his accomplishments, but of the admiration his stepson, James, began to show him. James's sudden wonderment with both Thomas and his career filled the hole that had been formed by our ice-cold loveless marriage. And that suited me just fine.

Thomas began playing a more active role in James's life. James, desperate for a father figure, clung to him with a fierce intensity, unable to see that he was merely feeding Thomas's insatiable ego. The arrangement was unsettling, but it worked. James thrived materially—his clothes became nicer, his gifts more extravagant, our vacations more opulent. Publicly, Thomas referred to James as his son, and James wore the title like a badge of honor. Together, we presented the picture-perfect family: school functions as a team, dinners as a unit, movie dates. By then, the double life I was living came to me as easily as breathing. In public and behind closed doors I was the picture-perfect wife. In private, I was absolutely dead inside.

On James's tenth birthday, I gave him a special edition box set of *The Lord of the Rings*. Beaming, I watched as he pulled out the first book, flipping through the pages with the reverence of someone holding a treasure.

"You really listened," he murmured, a small, almost shy smile forming on his lips.

"Of course I listened," I said, brushing a lock of white hair from his forehead. "I remember you telling me how you wanted to read the first book. Now you have the whole set."

He looked up at me, his brown eyes filled with warmth. James always just wanted to be *heard*. Then, he set the book aside and wrapped his arms around my waist, pressing his face into my side. I felt his body relax against mine, the way he had done when he was little, when he still fit perfectly curled against me during bedtime stories and scraped-knee consolations.

"Thank you, Mom," he whispered, and I felt my throat tighten.

I held him close, resting my chin on the top of his head. "Happy birthday, sweetheart."

For a moment, it was just us—the pages of the books between us, the weight of unspoken love in the space we shared. In that instant, before time had a chance to move forward and take him further away from me, I felt the warmth of the boy who still needed his mother.

Then, Thomas, always the showman, presented James with a sleek new cell phone. It had three preprogrammed contacts: Thomas, our home landline, and Eugene—James's birth father. With a flourish, Thomas told James he could reach out to Eugene whenever he wanted. Eugene had drifted out of James's life years earlier, ceasing visitation altogether. James's face lit up at the possibility of reconnecting with his birth father, and I felt a glimmer of hope. Maybe Thomas was finally accepting Eugene's role as a parental figure in James's life.

But Eugene never answered. Call after call, text after text—silence. I watched as the rejection chipped away at James's spirit. Having a father who wants nothing to do with you is a lot for a ten-year-old to process. Though he never admitted it, James felt abandoned. Soon, the sparkle in my son's eye vanished, and the bright, colorful designer clothing was replaced by black. The child-like wonder and resilience was replaced with negative self-talk. He became introverted and had trouble forming friendships in school. Even acting out and occasionally exploding in rage-like episodes. Worst of all, he began withdrawing from me.

I begged Thomas to intervene, to reach out to Eugene and demand an explanation. He promised he would. But nothing changed. Eugene remained silent, and James's despair deepened. My son was breaking before my eyes.

One day I decided I'd had enough. If Thomas wasn't going to act, I would. The next morning, I crept into James's room while he slept and took his phone from the nightstand. I snuck into the master closet—the one Thomas had claimed for himself after suggesting I use the guest room for my things. In the privacy of the small room, I dialed the number Thomas had programmed for Eugene.

The phone rang—and from somewhere in the closet, I heard a faint buzzing.

Confused, I followed the sound, uncovering a shoebox on the top shelf. Inside was a burner phone, its screen glowing with an incoming call. Next to it was a pistol. I froze, my breath hitching. The gun didn't shock me—it wasn't unreasonable for Thomas to have one to protect our family if necessary—but the secrecy of it unnerved me. Slowly, I replaced the weapon and picked up the phone.

My jaw dropped.

The number Thomas had given James, the one he claimed belonged to Eugene, was connected to this burner phone that Thomas had buried deep in the closet. The "gifted" cell phone had been a cruel calculated ploy to make James hate his real father and continue to worship Thomas—Thomas only.

The depth of my husband's manipulation took my breath away. Thomas hadn't just lied—he had orchestrated an elaborate betrayal, exploiting James's pain to feed his own ego. My hands trembled as I held the phone, staring into the darkness of the closet, feeling the weight of the truth suffocate me.

I could handle Thomas's manipulation when it was directed at me, but not my child.

I absolutely lost it.

Shaking with anger, I burst into the shop where Thomas was working on a piece for what would be his first-ever exhibit. I tossed the burner phone in front of him, sending it clattering onto the table.

"What the hell is this?" I snapped, heart pounding.

After recognizing the phone, Thomas slid the safety goggles onto the top of his head and looked at me.

"It's to protect James," he said, in that cool, calm tone that made me want to jump into oncoming traffic.

"*Protect him?*" I squealed.

"Yes." Slowly, he pushed away from the bench and stood. His large frame towered over me and I felt myself waver under his intimidation.

"Protect him from what?" I demanded, though my voice had begun to shake.

"From being disappointed by his deadbeat father."

"He's not disappointed by him." I took a step back. "He just wants a relationship—"

"*This* is his home, Emilia!" Thomas flung out his arms, missing hitting me by a mere inch. "James has everything he needs here. He doesn't need the mind-fuck of occasionally communicating with a father who doesn't even want him. Don't you see that? I'm doing what's best for James."

Before I could stop myself, the words came tumbling out. "Bullshit! You're jealous. You always have been. You're worried Eugene is going to inhibit your relationship. You are a narcissistic, jealous man who has to control and own everything in your life—including me, and now James."

A slow, crimson wave slid up Thomas's neck.

As he closed the inches between us, his hands curled to fists. "Some days you make me want to kill myself, do you know that?" He sneered in my face. "You *both* do. You and James. Then what would you do? You have no job. And for all your ungratefulness, you sure seem to enjoy all those Louis Vuitton handbags I've gifted you—and that ring on your finger, and the BMW in the garage, and the nails every two fucking weeks."

He lifted his chin, scowling down at me like I was nothing more than a bug stuck to the bottom of his shoe. "You're lucky I'm not walking on you—you and your ugly bastard son."

A sudden flash of movement pulled my attention to where James had been hiding behind the door.

He'd heard everything.

SEVENTEEN

EMILIA

Then

Two days before Thanksgiving, James was scheduled to meet Eugene. It was a meeting long overdue, driven by Eugene's sudden and unexpected desire to mend their fractured relationship. Over a year had passed since they'd last seen each other, and James, now twelve years old, was in the throes of wading through the more complex emotions of human existence.

Thomas approved the visitation without hesitation, which didn't surprise me. He had grown distant from James since James had overheard him mutter the unforgivable phrase: *"ugly, bastard son."* Their relationship, once strained, had become almost nonexistent. Every day I waited for divorce papers, while secretly stockpiling money every chance I could get, but then I realized that a divorce wouldn't match the perfect persona of Thomas's new famous lifestyle.

James was both nervous and excited about the visitation. He'd chosen his nicest black dress shirt to wear. By that time, James's wardrobe consisted of only black clothing.

Thirty minutes before we were set to leave, I came downstairs to find Thomas in the kitchen, his voice low but firm as he spoke into the phone.

"...No, I'm sorry. He's got a 104 temperature... I know, terrible timing. I'll let you know if he starts feeling better, but just plan the holidays without him for now. The doc said whatever's going around lasts about two weeks."

My stomach dropped as the pieces clicked into place.

I stormed into the kitchen just as Thomas hung up. My expression must have betrayed that I'd been listening because his eyes narrowed, gearing up for the inevitable confrontation.

"This has to stop," I hissed, stepping closer to him, my voice low so James wouldn't hear.

"Oh, I agree," Thomas shot back. "You eavesdropping? Yeah, that's gotta stop."

"No. I'm talking about your sick manipulation. I just heard you lie to Eugene."

"And?"

"*And?!* And it's not okay. This *has* to stop, Thomas."

"What does, exactly?"

"Your blatant disregard for James's well-being! You don't even like to be in the same room as him anymore!"

A vein in Thomas's neck began to pulse.

"I've tried," he hissed. "I've tried mending things with him. I suggested Boy Scouts, didn't I? I thought it could be something we could do together. I made the effort."

"You only suggested Boy Scouts because your buddy asked you to be a mentor with him. And besides, James didn't *want* to do Boy Scouts, Thomas. He told you that!"

"What boy doesn't want to do Boy Scouts?"

"Plenty of them," I shot back, my voice rising. "He's not you. He's his own person! He's almost a teenager—he has his own interests, his own likes and dislikes. Just because they don't mirror yours doesn't mean you can't bond with him." Heat surged up the back of my neck. "He's started painting, Thomas! He's an artist, just like you!"

"It's not the same," he muttered, shaking his head. "I do bladesmithing. That's not paint on paper."

"Are you hearing yourself? James is desperate for your approval. He's *screaming* for it. He's been trying to replicate Vincent van Gogh's paintings. He has a book hidden under his bed, along with his drawings. Go ask him about it. Show some interest."

Thomas crossed his arms, his gaze dark and menacing. "Why don't you ask him about it? He's drifted from you, too. You two barely talk anymore. And you're his *real* mother."

The words hit me like a slap in the face.

"Get out," I seethed, my body trembling. "Get the hell out of this house before I do something we'll both regret."

Thomas's face turned crimson, his eyes wild with a rush of fury. "This is my house, Emilia." He stepped closer, threatening. "And let's not forget—you've already done plenty to regret. Starting with the night you spread your legs for some redneck in a bar bathroom."

"Isn't that calling the kettle black? I know you've been cheating on me. I can smell that putrid vanilla perfume on you. Fuck you, Thomas. I'm leaving."

I spun around to leave but he grabbed my arm, his fingers digging in so hard I felt the skin break beneath his nails. He yanked me back, his breath hot against my face.

"You're not going anywhere, and *I'm* not going anywhere."

"You can't keep me here against my will," I snarled back. "James deserves a better life. A real father figure. Someone who loves him."

"His real father doesn't even love him." His grip tightened.

"At least he wants to see him."

"You will not leave this house, Emilia," Thomas whispered, shaking me so hard my teeth chattered. "And if you do, God help me, you won't return in one piece."

The next day Eugene died in a mysterious hunting accident.

EIGHTEEN
LUCY

Now

The shrill chime of the doorbell jolts me awake, its grating rendition of *The Stars and Stripes* slicing through the stillness of the night. My heart lurches as I sit up, disoriented with sleep. I must have fallen asleep while waiting for Emilia to do the same.

Beside me, Emilia doesn't stir.

Carefully, I edge off the bed and slide my glasses onto my face. The clock on the nightstand glows faintly: 12:15 a.m. Who could possibly be at the Caine residence at this hour?

My gaze drifts to the cluster of prescription bottles by the bedside, and a cold realization creeps over me. I must have slept through Mr. Caine administering Emilia's nightly dose. The thought of him moving about the room, working around my unresponsive body, fills me with an inexplicable unease.

The doorbell rings again.

"Dammit," I mutter, spinning on my heel and hurrying out of the room so that Emilia doesn't wake.

I jog down the staircase wearing an oversize T-shirt, mesh

shorts, and mismatched socks; my usual night clothes. My hair is tangled and frizzy, and I probably look like a gremlin.

The outside security lights illuminate the front porch where a silhouette paces back and forth.

Using the keypad, I punch in the security code that Consuelo gave me to disarm the alarm.

The bell rings again.

I yank open the door, biting back a hundred curse words.

"Who *the hell* are you?" the woman barks, blinking wildly, seemingly shocked and disgusted by me. "And what is wrong with your eyes?"

Affronted, I jerk back my chin. I thought I'd left the assholes back in Los Angeles.

"My name is Lucy," I respond calmly, although what I really want to do is punch the woman in the face. "I work here, and I was born with different-colored eyes. Who are you?"

By this point, I shouldn't be surprised that the woman standing before me is also beautiful. Unlike Emilia and Consuelo, she is no more than five feet tall, with wild, curly blonde hair, and a face frozen with injectables. She carries a large Louis Vuitton duffel bag. The iconic print matches the belt cinched around her waist. On her feet are a pair of bejeweled cowboy boots.

I hate her already.

"What do you mean, you work *here*?" The woman wags a long French-tipped nail at me.

It's then that I realize she is severely intoxicated. She repeats the question twice more, each time blowing the putrid scent of liquor into my face.

"Can I help you with something?" I cut in, seconds from slamming the door in her face.

"No, *you* absolutely cannot help me." The woman barges past me, sending a wave of cheap vanilla perfume into the air.

"*Hey.*" I grab her arm, a sudden—unexpected—protective-ness rushing me. Not of Mr. Caine or his home, but of Emilia.

Miniature Barbie spins around and raises her hand to strike me. My body braces for the blow, but the attack is thwarted by Mr. Caine's booming voice.

"Whoa, whoa, whoa!"

He sprints across the foyer, fully dressed in jeans and a dress shirt, despite it being past midnight.

"Meredith," he snaps. "*Stop it.* What are you doing here?"

Meredith?

I step back and unclench my fist, thankful I didn't punch her. I surely would have lost my job.

The woman is now laser focused on Mr. Caine, and not me, thank God.

"Who the hell is this?" she yells, flinging a hand in my direction.

Mr. Caine grabs her arm. "I asked what are *you* doing here?"

"Who. Is. *This?*" Again, she gestures to me.

"Jesus, Meredith." Mr. Caine shakes his head. "You are completely wasted." He looks at me, horrified. "I am *so sorry*, Lucy."

Although my heart is roaring in my chest, I nod and bite my tongue.

"This is my ex-wife," he says. "Please excuse her."

Ex-*wife?*

Though Mr. Caine is speaking to me, Meredith won't stop speaking over him, asking him who I am. The sudden rush of noise has my pulse skyrocketing. I wish Consuelo was here. She'd know what to do.

Mr. Caine grabs Meredith by her shoulders to calm her down. He explains that he has hired me to help with Emilia. At the mention of his (current) wife's name, Meredith's eyes narrow and glaze over like ice.

It becomes clear that I am standing in the middle of some sort of domestic or family issue.

"Again, I'm sorry," Mr. Caine apologizes while still holding onto Meredith. "I'm embarrassed. Please let me handle this. Give us a minute."

"Yes, of course." I awkwardly bow my head like a servant and step back. There's something about Mr. Caine that makes me feel less-than. More than his success and good looks, he has an air of power and confidence about him that I've always craved.

I'm way too curious about this new development to go back upstairs so, I make my way to the kitchen under the guise of getting a cup of tea. Once out of their line of sight, I sneak to the edge of the doorframe to eavesdrop, but it's no use. Thomas is speaking to Meredith aggressively—there's no mistaking that— but in a hushed manner. Between their arguing I can only make out one word:

Emilia.

Frowning, I press my back against the wall.

Mr. Caine has an ex-wife? What is she doing here? There was no mention of an ex-wife when I ran a Google search on him, and Consuelo didn't mention it either. I know that he and Emilia have been married for decades. So, this must have been a previous marriage? And he must have been very young.

Eventually, the voices in the foyer calm.

I peek around the corner as my boss and Meredith disappear down the hall, his hand resting on her lower back.

Well, this is interesting.

NINETEEN

EMILIA

Then

"Sit down, son."

Son. It was the first time Thomas had addressed James as "son" in years. The word hung in the air like a foreign object, heavy and awkward, as though Thomas himself wasn't sure how it fit into the conversation.

The thunderstorm drummed relentlessly on the roof, a steady, rhythmic pounding that mirrored the tension building in the room. I stood in the corner of the kitchen, stomach churning, doing everything I could to keep it together. I had to stay strong for James. He was about to fall apart, and he would need me when he did.

The headline was all over the evening news:

Local Man Dies in Tragic Hunting Accident.

I caught James's flickering glance, his eyes seeking reassurance, before he slowly settled into a chair at the kitchen table. Thomas sat across from him.

The house was deadly silent.

Thomas settled his gaze on James.

"Your birth father is dead."

James's eyes went wide, his face draining of color until he looked almost ghostly pale. My heart cracked for my son.

"Eugene is dead?" His voice sounded so small.

Thomas nodded, his expression solemn but sharp. "There was a terrible accident when he was hunting. A ricochet bullet—it's not uncommon, unfortunately. He was found late this morning."

A moment passed, heavy as a wet blanket.

"I'm in contact with Eugene's mother from Missouri," Thomas continued. "She actually has purchased some of my work before, so we already knew each other. Anyway, the funeral will be Wednesday. Would you like to go?"

James narrowed his eyes. "You're a liar."

The words came harsh and abruptly, cutting through the air like a knife. My stomach dropped at the unexpected response. The look on my son's face was unlike anything I'd seen before. He was no longer a boy—in that moment, he was a full-grown teenager enraged with both hatred and pain.

Thomas squinted, his jaw tightening as he leaned forward, placing his elbows on the table. "What did you just call me, boy?"

"I called you a liar because I don't believe you. I think you killed him."

"James, stop," I interjected, my voice urgent as I rushed across the kitchen, desperate to diffuse the situation.

Thomas flung out his hand, halting me in my tracks. "Stop! Let him speak."

James began trembling, his small hands clenching into fists at his sides. "I can see you're lying, and I think you killed him and made it seem like an accident. And, by the way, I am *not* an ugly bastard child." He surged out of his chair, knocking it backward sending it clattering onto the floor. Then, like a dam breaking, he began screaming at Thomas. "I hate you so much! I *hate* you!" Spittle flew from his lips. "You killed him! I hate you, I hate you, I hate you!"

Before I could react, Thomas was out of his chair, moving faster than I could. As I lunged forward to block him, he yanked me backward, sending me stumbling and falling onto the cold tiled floor.

Before I could get my footing, Thomas had James by the collar, his knuckles white as he gripped the fabric. James struggled but then began sobbing.

"You'd better never speak to me like that again, son," Thomas whispered through gritted teeth. "It would be a shame to lose your mother in a freak accident, just like you lost your dad, wouldn't it?"

TWENTY
LUCY

Now

I decide to *actually* make myself a cup of tea, considering I'm wide awake now, thanks to our unannounced drunken midnight visitor.

I'm pouring boiling water into a cup, staring out the pitch-black window, when I sense someone behind me. I spin around, sloshing piping-hot water on my socked foot.

"Sorry—I didn't mean to scare you," Mr. Caine blurts.

"No, it's okay," I squeak out, then wiggle my toe to confirm it's not melted. Then, I (carefully) slide the kettle back onto a potholder.

When I turn back, Mr. Caine is staring at me in that same strange, intense way as when we first met. It's unnerving. He should be used to my different-colored eyes by now.

"So," I say, breaking the odd tension that has suddenly filled the room. "That was..."

"I know. Weird and terrible." He sighs and rubs the back of his neck. "So, yeah, that's my ex-wife, Meredith Nichols. I'm so sorry."

"Yeah, she's, uh, something else."

"She's drunk. Very, very drunk. And again, I apologize; she should've never spoken to you like that. I talked to her about it, and trust me, it won't happen again. I'm very, very sorry." He scrubs his hands over his face. "What a rough start to your new job, huh?"

Better than sleeping in my car.

"It's fine. Please don't worry about it. Water under the bridge."

"Are you sure you're okay? I feel terrible."

"Yes, I promise, I'm fine."

Mr. Caine nods, then blows out a breath. "So... what kind of tea are you having?"

"Chamomile."

He pulls a face. "I can't stand chamomile."

"Then why do you have three tins of it in the pantry?"

He shrugs. "It's a trademark tea. Feel like I should."

"Does Emilia like it?"

"I..." He frowns. "Yes, I think she does. And, on that note, I think I'll have some tea, too. Take a break from the coffee."

His shoulder brushes against mine as he reaches into the pantry and grabs a tin of Earl Grey. "Always black for me." He winks.

"Even at midnight?"

"Especially at midnight." Mr. Caine picks a mug from the cabinet, lifts the kettle, and fills the mug to the brim. "I work best at night."

I take a step back to allow for distance between us. It's the first time I wonder if Mr. Caine would make a move on me, despite not being nearly as attractive as the other women in his life. There is something about him that is always on—always on "flirt," no matter who is on the receiving end. It's also strange that he's flipped a switch and simply turned off the drama that just happened in foyer.

I wonder if his apology was just for show so that I won't quit. Is he that desperate to be relieved of his wife?

I lean against the counter, and, unable to keep my mouth shut, ask, "So, where is she now?"

"Meredith?"

Of course Meredith. Who else would I be talking about?

"She'll be staying here tonight," he says.

My eyes pop with surprise. I wasn't expecting that. Meredith is drunk, of course Mr. Caine wouldn't let her drive—but I assumed that he would either drive her home himself or call a driver for her.

A moment lingers between us as my boss contemplatively dips his tea bag into the water.

"Meredith," he mutters, "has some problems. Aside from being an alcoholic, she has depression and anxiety."

"I could've guessed all that."

"Right? And that wasn't even a full-blown incident."

I watch him closely as he sips his tea, while I mentally weave more details into the ever-growing story of Thomas Caine.

"I gave Meredith her medicine"—another woman on medicine?—"and she should be out like a light soon. She'll stay here until she climbs out of this latest hole she's dug herself into. Probably two days."

Two days?

A million questions pummel my brain. Why doesn't Meredith have friends who can pick her up and take care of her? Or a husband? Or even a grown child? Is she married with a family of her own? Does her husband not care? And lastly, most disturbingly, why didn't Mr. Caine kick her out like I would hope any married man would do?

"You're judging me," he says, wincing.

"Sorry." I wrinkle my nose. "Busted. I am, yes."

He snorts. "You're blunt. I like you, you know that?"

Despite my distaste for Mr. Caine, I feel flattered.

"So, this is officially the sixteenth time this has happened over the years," he confesses. "Maybe more than that."

"*What?*" I almost drop my tea.

"Yep. Ever since we divorced decades ago—before I met Emilia, obviously—she's been doing this. Meredith finds herself on a drinking binge, goes crazy, and then drives to my house in a manic state."

"My God."

"I know. It's a lot."

"Why don't you...?"

"Call the cops?"

I nod.

"I have. The first five or six times it happened, I did. Emilia did too, on one occasion. But it keeps happening. And I'm not going to press charges on my ex-wife." He vehemently shakes his head. "I wouldn't do that. Anyway, she's been married three times after me. The first husband kicked her out for her drinking, and the last two left because she was still madly in love with me. This is according to the voicemails the men left me, anyway."

I begin twirling the tea bag around in my cup. Tea, *indeed*.

"And no, Lucy, it's not because I'm so fantastic—although I'd like to think so. It's my bank account. That's all she's interested in. Meredith and I married right out of high school and well before I made any money. We were young and dumb. The marriage lasted less than eighteen months. She," he uses air quotes, "'couldn't get over me' *after* I started making money. You see, Meredith barely graduated from high school. She has no college degree. She's been in and out of jobs her whole adult life. She's not really..."

Smart? What a dick.

He exhales. "It's sad. I feel sorry for her."

I feel sorry for your wife.

"Anyway," he sighs, "Meredith will sleep in the guest room next to my shop. You shouldn't have to mess with her. She'll be downstairs, and you'll be upstairs with Emilia. And again, I'm sorry you had to deal with this. I, uh…" He lifts his mug. "I need to get back to work."

Mr. Caine offers me a crooked smile and disappears down the hall.

I lean against the counter and sip my tea.

I consider Emilia sleeping on the second floor, and a wave of sadness comes over me. All these *women*.

Sick to my stomach, I pour my tea down the drain and begin the trek back upstairs with one question nagging my brain.

I wonder what Emilia thinks of me?

TWENTY-ONE
EMILIA

Then

The final straw was when I overheard Thomas tell James he'd hurt me if James ever disrespected him again. After that, I could no longer accept my husband's controlling, manipulative, vile behavior. That night, I packed a bag while Thomas was shut away in his shop, and at one in the morning, I woke up my eleven-year-old son.

Jame's sleepy eyes opened, blinking, trying to process what was happening.

"Shh," I'd cooed, putting my finger to my lips. "Get up, but be quiet."

"What?" he whispered, sitting up. His hair was sticking up at all ends, reminding me of when he was a toddler. "What's happening?"

The scent of his fruity shampoo and lived-in sheets made my heart swell. I loved him so damn much. I wanted to pick up him and put him in my pocket and keep his safe from all evils.

"We're leaving," I whispered back, swallowing the knot in my throat.

"We're leaving Thomas?"

"Yes."

Even in the darkness of the room, I could see the change in James's eyes. From curiosity and worry to understanding and courage. The same fearlessness as when he accused Thomas of killing his birth father. Chest puffed—and breaking my heart even more—James nodded, then hurried out of bed and dressed in the clothes I'd laid out for him.

Slanted rain and a bitter wind hit us like a tidal wave as we slipped out the back door.

"Where are we going?" James whispered, his voice trembling with the cold.

"Shh, just follow me," I murmured, glancing over my shoulder.

We ducked our heads against the rain, skirting the edge of the property line, careful to stay cloaked in the darkness. The bare trees above us swayed violently, their skeletal branches clawing at the night sky. Our sneakers sank into the soggy ground, soaking our socks and chilling us to the bone. Every few steps, I turned back, checking the dim glow of Thomas's shop windows, where dots of light flickered like distant watchful eyes.

I reached back and grabbed James's hand, his small, cold fingers clutching mine tightly as we slipped between the last two houses on the street. The *For Sale* sign of the last house creaked ominously in the wind, whipping back and forth on its rusty hinges.

Pulling the key fob from my pocket, I unlocked the BMW parked at the curb.

"Why is your car parked here?" James asked.

Yanking open the door, I ushered him inside gently but urgently. "Don't worry about it, sweetheart."

James didn't need to know about the risk I'd taken earlier—how, while Thomas was in the shower, I had crept into the garage, started the car, and quietly drove it down the street to park it out of earshot. He didn't need to know how long I had stood there in the dark, rain pattering against the hood, debating whether this plan was madness or survival. All he needed to know was that we were leaving, and we weren't looking back.

I tossed the backpack into the passenger seat and climbed behind the wheel, the cold leather biting through my soaked jeans. Hands on the steering wheel, I checked the rearview mirror. No sign of Thomas.

"Okay, honey, buckle up, please," I said, trying to keep my voice steady.

Once I heard the soft *click* of the seatbelt, I pressed the ignition, and the engine roared to life.

With one final glance at the empty street behind us, I put the car in gear and drove off into the storm.

"Mom, what are we doing?"

"Shh, honey—just give me a few seconds, please."

A few seconds to calm my racing heart while I checked the rearview mirror every five seconds, half-expecting to see Thomas barreling down the road after us.

Twenty minutes later, we merged onto the interstate. *Finally.* After checking the rearview one last time, I allowed myself to exhale and loosen the death grip I'd had on the steering wheel.

"Okay, we can talk now. Thank you for giving me a moment."

"I'm proud of you, Mom."

I looked at James in the mirror. His face was strong, resolute, his chin lifted in defiance as he stared back. And once again—for far too many times—he looked eleven going on forty.

I blinked away the tears threatening to sting my eyes. "Thank you—and I'm proud of you."

"Why are you leaving him?"

"It was time."

"Good. He's an asshole, Mom."

"James, I do not like that language."

"It fits."

"Fair point." I sighed. "Okay. Here's the plan. We're going to drive through the night and all day tomorrow and then find a nice little bed and breakfast to stay in for a few days while I make a plan."

I had roughly five thousand dollars I'd secretly stashed away over the last few years. Barely enough to get us through this escape and into decent lodging while I searched for a job.

"He killed Eugene, Mom. I know he did."

"How do you know?"

"I just do."

"A gut feeling?"

"Yeah."

"And what do I say about gut feelings?"

"Always, *always* trust them."

"That's right. But with this situation, James, we have to let it go. It doesn't mean you have to change what you believe happened, but it does mean that we have to understand it does us no good to investigate our claims. The police have already declared it an accident. And for all we know it was an accident. And also, don't ever forget, the chief and Thomas are childhood friends."

"What do you mean?"

"I mean, Chief Bobby and Thomas grew up together, and friends protect each other. I'm an outsider with no ties to the community. No one would believe me if I told them Thomas had something to do with Eugene's death. Add to that Thomas has become a local celebrity and everyone fucking loves him."

"Mom, I do not like it when you use that language."

"Sorry." I smirked at James's grin in the rearview mirror. "It fits."

"Was Thomas home when it happened?" he asked.

"Because if we could prove he was gone the morning Eugene died…"

"I don't know, honey. He's been living in his shop the last week. He could have come and gone and I would have had no idea."

"Don't you *want* to know?"

"Absolutely not. James, hear me. Sometimes you have to let things go. Leave them in the past, and begin a new chapter."

"Like we're doing right now?"

Before I could answer, blue and red lights lit up behind us.

My heart jumped into my throat. I knew I wasn't speeding.

"Mom!" James squeaked, scared.

"It's okay—everything is okay," I said, trying to still my shaking voice while I pulled onto the shoulder.

"Mom, I'm scared."

Me too.

Through the foggy rear windshield, I watched the large, black silhouette emerge from the patrol car behind us. The officer moved with an unsettling calm, each step deliberate, heavy boots splashing through puddles as the downpour blurred his form.

The flashlight in his hand cut through the sheets of rain, casting flickering beams across the soaked pavement. I clenched the steering wheel tighter, my knuckles whitening.

The officer stopped at my window. Water streamed off the brim of his campaign hat, obscuring his face in shadow. After shining the light inside the cab, blinding me, he tapped on the glass.

"Yes, sir?"

Raindrops pelted the interior of my car as I rolled down the window.

"Get out of the vehicle, please, ma'am."

"No, Mom!" James whisper-hissed from the backseat,

igniting a motherly instinct to protect my son so fierce I felt my muscles tense into fight mode.

"Officer, my son is in the back. He's scared. Can you just tell me why you're pulling me over?"

"Ma'am, I don't want to have to ask again. Get out of the car."

Panic flooded my system.

I looked back at James, as his eyes filled with tears. My heart shattered into a million pieces. What awful things this boy had witnessed already in his life. What kind of mother was I? Running away with him, trying to explain everything as if his little head would understand. What kind of life was I forcing him to live? We'd be poor, no question about it. He'd have to go to a new school, make new friends. Watch me struggle while I worked two jobs to make ends meet. I'd be absent from his life, fighting to pay the bills. Could I even afford a sitter?

Was I doing this for him—or me? Was I dragging my son through the dirt just so that I could be happy?

"Everything is okay, sweetheart," my voice cracked. "I just need to get out of the car for a second. Stay here. I'll be right back."

My knees were shaking so badly I could hardly stand. I left the car door open—uncaring that the interior was getting soaked —so that James felt less alone.

Just then, another pair of headlights cut through the rain. This one an unmarked truck. A short, burly man got out. Cowboy hat, thick jacket, cowboy boots. Chief Bobby Dunlap. Thomas's childhood friend.

"Emilia," Bobby cooed in a condescending, placating voice. "Sorry about this." He turned to the officer. "Give us a second, will ya?"

"What the hell is going on?" I asked, as the officer disappeared to the back of my car.

"We've got a BOLO out for you."

"A be-on-the-lookout? For what? Why?"

"Your husband believes you're a suicide risk."

My insides turned to water. I couldn't speak. A *suicide* risk?

Beside us, the other officer had popped open my trunk.

"Thomas called me after realizing you snuck out and took James with you. He's worried about you—and James."

My jaw unhinged. There was no mistaking the implication. That I would hurt not only myself, but also James.

The chief continued. "Thomas told me about your breakdown after you found out that Eugene died. He told me you'd been mad at him for disowning James, and mad at yourself for getting involved with him in the first place. And how you got so upset you threatened to kill yourself." He put his swollen arthritic hand on my shoulder. "I'm sorry for your loss."

My loss? Eugene and I didn't have a relationship—unless Thomas had told them otherwise. I wanted to set the record straight, to tell the chief he had it all wrong. That it wasn't me who was volatile—it was Thomas. Thomas, who once told me he wanted to kill himself. Thomas, who had the real issues. He was the manipulative abuser in our marriage, not me.

But I knew better than to try. He wouldn't believe me. No one would. I didn't have the bruises or broken bones to show for it, no physical evidence of the damage Thomas had inflicted.

The sharp *clunk* of the officer rooting through my trunk jarred me back to the present. I swallowed hard, trying to steady the storm of emotions churning inside me.

"So..." The chief clapped his hands together, spewing raindrops in my face. "I'm going to need you to take yourself, and your son, back home."

"No," I snapped, beginning to lose control. "Absolutely not. I've left my husband and I have no legal obligation to return home."

"You're right, unless we believe you—*or your son*—are in immediate danger or that you're mentally incapacitated."

"Mentally incapacitated?!"

He nodded, solemnly, like I was a poor, fragile woman who didn't know what was best for her.

"Got it!" the officer yelled from behind my opened trunk. He held up a gun, wrapped in cellophane paper. I recognized it immediately. Everything suddenly became crystal clear.

The gun the officer had just found in my trunk was the same one I'd found in Thomas's closet, next to the burner phone that was linked to Eugene's number. The same gun that he would have used to kill Eugene, if he did it—and the gun that had *my* prints all over it. And Thomas would have known that, too, because he knew I would have examined the gun when I found the burner phone next to it.

I felt like the world was closing in on me. I was so shocked, so confused, so dumbfounded that I couldn't think straight. I looked at James in the backseat, teary-eyed, trembling in fear.

My son.

My beautiful, innocent, son. Who would he have if I was framed for murder?

My son did not deserve this.

I lifted my chin to meet the chief's gaze.

"Fine. If you promise to leave us alone, right now, I will willingly return home, with my son. You can call Thomas and tell him I'm on my way and that I won't leave again."

Because I knew exactly what my husband intended to do with that gun. Blackmail me for the rest of my life.

That night I made a decision to stay with Thomas, to stay in my cage of marriage.

A decision *for my son*. To give my life for his.

I didn't think things could get worse.

I was wrong.

TWENTY-TWO
LUCY

Now

I'm lying in bed when I hear the creak of floorboards outside my room. The clock on the nightstand reads 2:47 a.m.

I sit up, certain it's not Emilia herself, because the steps are coming from the opposite end of the hall. And also, Emilia can't walk without assistance.

I regret not crawling back into bed with Emilia after the chaos downstairs. But I didn't want to risk Thomas tiptoeing around me again to give Emilia her medicine. The thought of it creeps me out. I also didn't want to wake up Emilia and risk her somehow finding out that Meredith is sleeping in her house.

Straining to see through the darkness, I squint at the cracked door. For a moment I think I see a pale face peeking through the crack, but just like that, it's gone.

The footsteps stop. I hold my breath.

A few seconds pass.

Thirty.

Could I have imagined the noise?

Hesitantly, I lie back down. But I surge up once again. I need to check on Emilia.

After ripping off the covers, I tiptoe to the door, avoiding the creaking floorboards I've made mental notes of.

When I peek outside, Meredith is standing in the doorway of Emilia's room, her back to me, frozen in place, staring inside. The dim light from Emilia's night lamp casts her in an eerie glow, her curly blonde hair frizzed into a halo-like outline. She's wearing an obnoxious pink pajama set donned with horseshoes and martini glasses—because of course she is.

A rush of protectiveness surges through me.

I don't like Meredith. For obvious reasons, considering the woman almost slapped me across the face, but also, I get a terrible vibe from her. Like when you pass a lone man in a dark alley at night. There's something unnerving in her wild, surly eyes.

I watch her for a minute, unsettled by what is happening. Meredith isn't moving or speaking. She is simply standing in the doorway like a ghost, where her ex-husband's wife sleeps.

I battle with what to do. Ignoring this odd behavior and returning to bed isn't an option, so I have to address it. I am Emilia's keeper, after all.

I step into the hallway and clear my throat.

Meredith doesn't flinch.

I clear it again, loudly enough that it's jarring in the silence.

Still, the woman doesn't turn around.

"Meredith," I whisper-hiss, stepping deeper into the hallway.

This time, Meredith turns her head slowly, offering me her profile. Her face is devoid of expression. Flat, dead. She is neither embarrassed nor surprised at my arrival. Or is it that she simply doesn't care?

"Meredith, can I help you with something?"

"Emilia is in my bed," she says matter-of-factly.

"I thought Thomas gave you a room downstairs." I join Meredith in the doorway. Emilia is asleep on her back, the night light illuminating her closed eyes. She looks like Sleeping Beauty, her hands folded on her stomach, her face serene.

"He did." Meredith refocuses on Emilia. "But this is supposed to be *my* room."

When I ran a psychic shop in downtown Los Angeles, dealing with unstable women was a daily occurrence. It was easy—give them advice, take their money, and walk them out the door. The difference now is that I am not in my own territory. I am not the boss. I have no authority here, and therefore, I'm finding it difficult to navigate this strange situation I've found myself in.

Meredith tilts her head to the side. "What did you think when you first met Emilia?"

I feel uncomfortable speaking about Emilia when she's ten feet away. I'm aware that Emilia could be pretending to sleep anytime her eyes are closed. That's what I would do. I would get so sick of living in a world where I couldn't react.

Choosing my words carefully, I say, "I haven't been able to connect with her yet."

Meredith snorts. "Good luck with that. Even if she was normal, it would be nearly impossible."

"What do you mean?"

"Emilia is someone who only shows what she wants you to see. Everything about her is a façade. A fake."

Fake?

"She's wrong for Thomas," Meredith continues, her disdain evident. "He's a creative person, an artist with a vision. He has such drive and ambition. He could never count on Emilia. She was never there for him."

"Losing a son can change a person," I say, defending the woman who can't speak for herself.

Meredith's eyes twinkle like a cat's. "No, honey, it's been

like this from day one. Long before he went away." She looks at me. "James ran away—from *her*."

"What do you mean, *from her?*"

"Stick around long enough, and you'll find out."

Is that a threat?

"What do you mean, Meredith? Do you know what happened to her son?"

Meredith snorts like a petulant teenager. "Why don't you ask her?"

I roll my eyes, annoyed. The million questions I have about Emilia's son will get nowhere with this drunken woman.

"Maybe I should go get Mr. Caine," I say impatiently.

"No," Meredith snaps. "Never interrupt Thomas while he's working. *Ever*."

"Well, is there something I can get you to help you go back to sleep?" In other words: *Get the hell out of here, crazy lady*.

"No, dear, you go on back to sleep now." Meredith offers me a creepy, doll-like smile that doesn't reach her eyes. "Go on."

I hesitate but then turn away. But instead of going to bed, I close my bedroom door just enough to hide behind it. I cross my arms over my chest, lean against the frame, and settle in to watch Meredith. To ensure she does not set one foot into Emilia's bedroom.

Five minutes pass, then ten.

Twenty.

Thirty.

Meredith never moves. And despite all her crazy behavior, I get the feeling that Meredith isn't nearly as dim-witted as Mr. Caine thinks she is.

TWENTY-THREE
EMILIA

Then

At 7:48 a.m. on March 9, 2005, seventeen-year-old James Caine left his home to go to school. He was never seen or heard from again.

"Does your son have any identifiable marks on his body? Like tattoos or birthmarks?"

"No."

A bead of sweat rolled down my back. The multi-colored kaftan I was wearing was damp against the kitchen chair. I cursed the nervous, haywire state I was in, responsible for making me sweat, even though our home was kept at a precise sixty-eight-degree temperature. I glanced at my husband who was pacing the kitchen like a caged animal.

"How about a beard?" the police officer pressed, regaining my attention. "Mustache, sideburns?"

"No."

Although Officer Barrett Jackson and I had only just met, I'd already labeled him as incompetent. He was a baby, mid-twenties, with rust-colored facial hair and a cartoonish square chin. Atop his head sat a beige cowboy hat, a bit crooked. Our hillbilly small-town police department sent a rookie cop to assist in the worst day of my life. Although I guess I should have been grateful.

At least this officer didn't know who I was. Everyone had heard about me "running away" with James in the middle of the night, after Eugene died. Overnight, I became the town crazy lady, and I'd held onto that title all these years later.

Impatient, I pushed the picture of my son I'd already provided across the table. "No identifiable marks, as you can see."

It was his Rock Hill High School picture. In it, my son was smiling, though it didn't quite reach his brown eyes. His white-blond hair was mussed. His collar was wrinkled as if he'd pulled his shirt from his backpack.

My gut twisted. I looked away.

Our attention whipped in the direction of something clattering to the floor in another room. Thomas lunged toward the doorway. The officer and I pushed back from the kitchen table and surged to our feet.

"Sir." Jackson gently grabbed Thomas's arm. "Please let the officers conduct their search."

Thomas whirled around, and for a moment I thought he was going to strike the officer. *Do it,* I thought. *Show everyone who you really are.*

"I don't understand why they have to search the *entire* house? Who approved this?"

"I did," I responded tartly, emboldened by the presence of law enforcement.

Thomas shot me a look of vile hatred, then refocused on the officer. "What are they looking for, anyway? And why haven't you called in the Georgia State Police yet? My stepson is *missing.*"

I was in awe of my husband, how easily he could play the part.

"I understand, Mr. Caine, and as I said before, we're looking for anything that can help point us in the direction of your missing stepson. I know it's uncomfortable—"

"*Uncomfortable?*" Thomas snorted. "Complete strangers are wandering my home. I told you, there isn't anything in the house that will tell you where he is. James left for school and never came—"

"That's *enough*, Thomas," I snapped, losing it.

I turned back to Jackson. This time, however, we didn't sit. The officer was keeping one eye on the loose cannon that was my husband.

"Mrs. Caine—"

"I told you already, please, call me Emilia."

"Emilia—sorry. I'm going to ask you a few personal questions about your son. They might sound odd at first, but please understand these help us build a picture of where he might have gone. Does James smoke?"

"Yes. I found cigarettes in his coat pocket a few months ago."

"Okay, do you know if James does any recreational drugs, in addition to cigarettes?"

"I don't think—"

"No," Thomas barked, clearly offended by the question. "My stepson doesn't do drugs."

By his expression, Officer Jackson wasn't taking our word on the no-drugs thing, but he didn't argue. After all, teenagers who smoke are significantly more likely to use drugs compared to those who don't smoke. Thomas wouldn't know this. He didn't know much about raising a child.

Jackson studied his notes. "Let's talk about his friends."

"I've already given you their names," I said. "James is very introverted. He prefers to be alone."

Thomas was now popping his knuckles one by one, each pop like a gunshot echoing off the walls. I was about to jump out of my skin.

"What about his birth father?"

A flicker to Thomas. "He's dead."

"Ah, that's right. Hunting accident a few years ago." The officer tapped his pen against the paper. "Speaking of hunting, what are James's hobbies?"

"He likes to paint."

Jackson appeared surprised by this. I imagined his offspring spent their spare time roping pigs in the backyard.

"What does he paint?"

"Abstract images, mostly. Colorful things."

Chaos on canvas. Those were my exact thoughts the moment I saw my son's first painting. Haphazard lines of color, melting together into a dizzying kaleidoscope. A rainbow of teenage angst, right there on canvas.

"Any signs of depression?"

I hesitated. "He... lately, James has been exceptionally quiet."

"What was his attitude when he left for school this morning?"

Tears stung and I quickly choked them back. *Never let them see you cry. They already think you're an emotional basketcase.*

"He was normal. But... ah..." Thomas's gaze bore into me. "He did, um, he did tell me he loved me."

A moment of silence settled in the room.

"Does your son always tell you he loves you before he leaves for school?"

"No." My stomach was twisting so viciously now that I might be sick.

The officer scrutinized Thomas, who had stopped pacing and was now staring at a spot on the floor. The tension felt like a fourth presence in the room.

"Emilia, let me ask you this. Is there any reason James would want to run away?"

"No," Thomas said, before I could answer. "He has a stable family, a nice house. We give him the space he needs when he needs it. He has it better than most kids his age."

"Okay," Jackson nodded. "So if you feel confident that he didn't run away, do you think something happened to him? That he was kidnapped?"

I flinched at the word. A mother's worst nightmare.

"I don't know what I think!" Thomas bellowed. "I'm answering all of your bullshit questions when instead you should be out looking for my stepson."

Stepson. Again with the bullshit act. My nails dug into my palms.

"We have to gather information first," Jackson remained calm.

"I'm calling Bobby." Thomas frantically searched the counter for his phone.

"He's uh—you know he retired last year. He's no longer the chief."

"Yeah, I know," Thomas snapped back. Blowing out a breath of frustration, Thomas gave up the search, knowing that his friend, the former police chief, could do nothing to help him now. After all, he'd done enough already, hadn't he?

"I promise you," Jackson continued, "we have a team already working on it, sir."

Just then, another young officer strode into the room, breaking the mounting tension. Perez. Another city cop, new.

We turned our attention to him.

Perez read from a small pocket notebook in his hand. "The local hospitals have been called—no one under the name James Caine has been admitted. The chief is currently working to obtain access to James's cell phone from the phone company.

From that, we're hoping to pin his location and also read his texts."

Thomas looked at me. I looked away.

The officer continued. "I have Suzie getting the CCTV footage of the school now to confirm he never showed." Perez closed the notebook and stuffed it into his pocket. Unlike Baby-Boy Jackson, this officer exuded both confidence and competency. "Door-to-door will begin within thirty minutes."

"What's door-to-door?" I asked.

"We're going to ask the neighbors if they've seen James or his car." Perez's phone rang and he disappeared out the front door.

Jackson refocused on me. I steeled myself for the question we'd all been waiting for him to ask.

"Mrs. Caine, I mean, Emilia"—he cleared his throat—"has there been any family drama lately?"

"No." Thomas spoke for the both of us.

Jackson nodded. He didn't believe my husband.

He shouldn't.

TWENTY-FOUR
LUCY

Now

After Meredith finally returns downstairs, I crawl into bed with Emilia to ensure I wake if she stirs, or if anyone else comes to the room. The thought of Emilia finding out her husband's ex-wife is here makes me sick to my stomach. I can't—won't—let that happen.

The room is cloaked in shadows, broken only by the dim, bluish glow of the moonlight spilling through the half-closed blinds. I lay on my side, the thick duvet pulled up to my chest, my eyes wide open, unable to sleep. Beside me, Emilia sleeps.

I wonder what it's like being locked in a body that refuses to move as it used to, refuses to speak, refuses to give her the freedoms I take for granted. To be trapped in this stillness, hearing the world move around her but never being able to engage with it.

The thought chills me.

I close my eyes for a moment, trying to imagine it. My muscles twitch involuntarily, and I wonder if she ever dreams of moving—if, in her mind, she runs and dances and stretches, only to wake up to this same unyielding stillness.

A light breeze from the open window stirs the curtains, carrying with it the cool, damp scent of night.

"Hey, Emilia," I whisper softly, though I know she can't answer. Her eyes flicker slightly, and for a brief second, her lips part and I think she's going to speak.

"Tell me your story," I whisper. "What happened?"

Tell me about your son, about Thomas, about Meredith, about the almost-divorces, about the stroke. I want to know it all.

But I'm met with silence.

I reach out, hesitating for a moment before gently resting my hand on her thin, papery forearm. I don't know why I do it—maybe to remind her that she isn't alone. Maybe to remind myself.

Keeping my fingertips on her arm, I turn onto my back, staring up at the ceiling, tracing the moonlight along the exposed beams.

I don't know if she feels my presence. I don't know if it matters. But I stay, because if I were her, I think I'd want someone lying beside me too, even if they couldn't fix anything.

But I want to fix it. So badly, I want to help this woman.

I will, I think. I will help her. Then, I close my eyes and pretend to sleep.

TWENTY-FIVE
EMILIA

Then – Six Years After James Went Missing

Behind me, the *tick, tick, tick* of the clock echoed in the silence, relentless and maddening. I didn't need to look to know it was well past midnight. Another sleepless night. Another endless vigil in this purgatory of waiting.

My hand trembled as I lifted my wine glass and took a mindless sip while my eyes scanned the scattered mess of notes, Post-its, and maps strewn across the desk. Each scribbled line represented a dead end, a glimmer of hope that had slipped through my fingers.

5/10: *George Liberty Park—possible sighting.*

5/10: *3:30 p.m. Blue Accord spotted at Wal-Mart parking lot in Black Hope. Security cameras confirmed not his. (Change license plate?)*

5/14: *Horseshoe Bar, Springdale—possible sighting with a young woman, blonde hair (??). Contacted Paula (old gf with* *blonde hair)—she denied it. Lying? Dig into socials. Talk to friends again?*

The police gave up months ago. They told me there was nothing more they could do, that missing persons cases like this tend to go cold. But I refused to let it go cold. I couldn't—I *wouldn't*. I would search until my last breath. Follow every lead, chase down every shadow.

Every day felt like dragging myself through a fog so dense I could hardly breathe. I tortured myself with questions: Was it my fault? What if I had done that, or this, would things be different? Did I let him down? Was he crying out for me right now? The guilt was a gnawing presence in my chest, hollowing me out from the inside.

I picked up a crumpled note that included dates and locations of all the places I'd contacted in my search for James.

My gaze fixed on the entry for Gold Loans.

Before I could talk myself out of it, I stood abruptly, my legs wobbling slightly as I grabbed my hoodie and slid into my slippers. After glancing at the clock—1:14 a.m.—I tiptoed through the house, careful not to make a sound.

As I passed Thomas's shop, the eerie whine of his so-called "creativity music" seeped through the cracked door. It wasn't music—it was some high-frequency tone that was supposed to boost focus and energy. I hated it.

Pausing for a moment, I peeked through the door's narrow opening. Thomas sat rigid at his workbench, his back to me, perfectly still. For a brief moment, I was pulled back in time, to the early years of our marriage. To me, waking in the middle of the night, tiptoeing into our teeny tiny living room and wrapping my arms around the shoulders of my new husband. Often, we would make love right then, right there on the floor under the ear lobe he painted me for our wedding gift. We were so happy then. We laughed hard. We loved harder.

A pang of sadness clogged my throat. Those days were long gone. Now, we barely spoke. We lived in separate worlds—mine revolving around finding James, his around pretending to move on. I didn't know this man anymore. I didn't love him. I didn't trust him. And I certainly didn't respect him.

Quietly, I backed away and slipped outside into the cold night. The stars above were dull and muted behind thin cloud cover. It reminded me of James's last painting—a replica of *Starry Night Over the Rhône*. It was good. I had been so proud of him.

My heart pounded as I drove through the empty streets, the flickering lampposts casting eerie shadows across the deserted sidewalks. The shops were closed, every house dark with sleep. I couldn't remember the last time I'd slept. I shouldn't even be driving, but it didn't matter. Nothing mattered except finding James.

I slowed as I approached Gold Loans, peering through the fogged windows. The pawn shop was one of the few businesses operating twenty-four-seven due to the nearby casino. Condensation blurred the glass, but I didn't see any customers inside.

Looping around the back, I parked in the shadows. My hands shook as I killed the engine and pocketed my keys.

Do it. Do it. You're his only advocate. Do it.

The mantra echoed in my mind as I stepped into the bitter wind, pulling up my hood to shield my face. My house shoes scuffed against the pavement, kicking aside loose gravel and dead leaves. I realized, with a flicker of detached amusement, that I'd forgotten to put on a bra. As if that was my biggest concern.

Steeling myself, I pulled open the door and stepped inside. Lisa, perched behind the counter, looked up from beneath her signature owlish glasses. Her expression immediately soured.

"Aw, shit," she muttered, her southern drawl thick with irritation.

I strode to the front desk, pulling a photo of James from my pocket. "I'm just checking—have any gold compasses come in recently? And have you—"

"Earl! Get out here, she's back!"

"Please," I pressed on, desperation creeping into my voice. "I know you've told me before, but I just need to check again—"

Lisa cut me off, her tone sharp. "Mrs. Caine, we've told you —like ten times now—we don't have anything. We haven't seen your son and if we get a gold compass we'll call you. You're drunk again, aren't you?"

Earl appeared from the back room, his expression hardened. "Goddammit, Emilia. I warned you after last time—I'll call the cops if you keep this up."

"No," I whispered, panic rising in my chest. That was the last thing I needed. The entire town now thought I was a suicidal crazy lady, which honestly, didn't feel too far from the truth.

"Please don't," I begged. "I just... I just need to know if anyone's seen my son."

"You need help, Emilia," Earl said, his voice tired. "Real help. Not booze, or pills. You need to see a head doctor."

I opened my mouth to argue, but my words twisted into a frustrated scream—a raw, guttural sound that tore through the quiet. "Everyone has given up! No one is looking for him anymore—don't you understand? I *have* to look! I'm the only one left! I'm the only one who cares!"

The next hour was a blur, except for one thing that is crystal clear and forever etched in memory: the look on Thomas's face as he glowered down at me on the floor tucked into the fetal position, sobbing and hugging my knees to my chest, while Lisa held me down.

TWENTY-SIX
EMILIA

Then

I didn't wake up one day and decide I was done. It wasn't a single moment or a dramatic revelation—though there have been many of both throughout our marriage. It was a slow awakening of the erosion of my life.

After James went missing, everything changed. I went into a deep, deep depression. I didn't care about anything other than finding my son. When Thomas told me he wanted to leave Rock Hill and build a new house out in the middle of nowhere. I said okay. I didn't care. When we moved in and he suggested that the first floor be his, and the second mine, I said great.

Each morning, I would wake up to a suffocating emptiness that made me want to stay in bed forever. The idea of facing another day was overwhelming. It felt like I was walking through a fog that never lifted. There were days when I didn't shower, didn't eat, didn't even try to hide the dark circles under my eyes. I was a ghost, moving through life without purpose, without connection.

My son had been the sole reason I'd stayed in my marriage.

I stayed because Thomas offered financial security that I couldn't, and then I stayed because of fear that Thomas would falsely accuse me of murdering Eugene. After all, my prints were all over the gun, and I'd gone "crazy," according to the gossips. Everything I did was for James. But when that piece of the puzzle was gone, I was left with nothing but being married to a man who thrived on control, who fed off manipulation, and who saw my forgiveness as weakness.

A man who was cheating on me left and right.

It took years, but eventually, I decided that spending my life in jail would be better than spending my life as this man's prisoner.

My body tensed as I felt him enter the bathroom.

"Emilia."

I didn't turn immediately. Instead, I shut off the shower slowly, allowing the last drops of water to patter onto the tile. Opening the glass door, I reached for the robe hanging nearby and slipped into it without a rush. The damp fabric clung to my skin as I stepped onto the floor mat, water pooling at my feet. When I finally faced him, Thomas stood there, a brown manila envelope clutched tightly in his grip. I didn't need to ask what it was. I already knew. The divorce papers I had him served at his latest local art exhibit.

"Did you really think I wouldn't file for divorce again, Thomas?" I asked, my voice cold, detached. I felt nothing—not anger, not sadness, not regret.

"I thought you'd talk to me about it first, like last time."

"There's nothing left to say," I replied, my tone flat. "We talked plenty after I caught you checking into the casino hotel last month with Whore Number Three—or was it Four? And we talked even more after your ex-wife Meredith showed up drunk on our doorstep—again. And you let her stay—*again*."

He opened his mouth to speak but I cut him off.

"No." I held up my hand. "We're so far past talking, Thomas. I'm done with everything."

His jaw clenched as he closed the inches between us. "I thought you'd learned by now that when you signed on the dotted line to be my wife, there was no going back."

I threw open my arms, exposing my bony, emaciated naked body through the slit of the robe. "I don't care!" I screamed in his face. "I don't care about anything anymore. Kill me; fuck, I don't care, Thomas! Don't you see that?"

"You're not leaving me, Emilia. You know that. I know what this is really about."

"About you sneaking off to the Department of Health to get a death certificate for our missing son without telling me? Or is it about you doing it so you could cash out the life insurance policy on him?"

"Emilia, it's been over fifteen years!" Thomas bellowed. "After seven years, a missing person can be legally declared dead. You know that."

"I know what presumption of death means, Thomas!" My voice echoed off the tiled walls. "Unlike you, I know every law, every statistic, every single fact about missing persons."

"How long are you going to keep doing this?" he snapped back. "Even if James isn't dead, he obviously doesn't want to be found. He doesn't want to be with us. Isn't that enough for you to stop looking for him?"

I let out a cold, bitter laugh. "And why do you think that is, Thomas? Why do you think James wouldn't want to be a part of this family? Go ahead, say it."

"Fuck you, Emilia."

"Fuck me?" I repeated, jabbing my finger into his chest, willing him to strike me. Hell, to kill me. Put an end to my misery. "That would be a change, wouldn't it? After all you've fucked every woman in town by now. I've endured your lies, your affairs, your manipulation, your pathetic apologies. No more. I deserve better than you—and *James* deserved better than you."

Like a flash of lightning, Thomas wrapped his hand around my throat.

He yanked me to him.

"You say that one more time and you will be spending the rest of your life in jail."

My nostrils flared as I gasped for breath.

He squeezed tighter, lowing his face inches from mine.

"I still have the gun, Emilia. With your prints all over the hilt, and also on the box of bullets that I used to shoot him with. The police kept the bullet casings from the scene. All I have to do is take the gun and box up there and they'll match the bullet that killed Eugene to the box with your prints." Tiny black spots began to cloud my vision. "I also have more letters you sent him —ones that I typed, pretending to be you. In them, you and Eugene get into an argument after he'd asked to borrow money from us. In the final letter, you agreed to a sum amount, and agreed to meet him—the morning he died."

Thomas's nails dug into my throat as the world began to spin. "You see, Emilia, no matter how many times you try, you're never going to get away from me. I always—*always*—win."

TWENTY-SEVEN
LUCY

Now

I am dead tired. Like, *can-hardly-keep-my-eyes-open* tired. After being unable to sleep thanks to Meredith's creepy late-night visit to the master bedroom, I was woken by Emilia's movement monitor going off at five-thirty.

I've guided Emilia to her favorite armchair facing the window, where the morning light spills across her lap in soft golden streaks. I tuck the knitted blanket around her legs—her favorite, the one she absently smooths with her fingertips when she thinks no one is watching. She hums in quiet approval as I set a bowl of oatmeal in front of her—organic, per the notes—though she still makes a face when she takes the first bite. I smile. "I know, I know. But it's good for you." Emilia doesn't respond, but the slight narrowing of her eyes tells me she has an opinion on that.

After breakfast, I settle beside her with the new book we picked out yesterday, this one a thriller promising "jaw-dropping" twists. We'll see. As I read, I feel Emilia's gaze on me, steady and searching, like she has before. At first, I assume she's just listening, tracking the rhythm of my voice, but when I glance over, she's watching me with an intensity that makes me pause.

Her expression is thoughtful, her brow faintly furrowed, like she's trying to read my soul.

Slowly her lips press together in the closest thing to a smile I've seen from her. It's fleeting, delicate, but it's there. And then, as if she's made up her mind about something, she reaches for my hand, her fingers cool and tentative against mine.

I don't pull away. Instead, I give her hand a gentle squeeze and return to the book, my voice softer now.

As I continue reading, she leans back in her chair, but her fingers remain curled loosely around mine.

It's now ten in the morning and the house remains quiet. I assume Meredith is still passed out downstairs, but I'm surprised Mr. Caine hasn't visited his wife yet. Emilia's medication schedule has become alarmingly sporadic, and I don't like this. Once my role in the home becomes more solidified, I'm going to request to take over her medications. I shudder to think of how little Emilia was taken care of before I arrived.

Emilia is staring out the window, her fingernail slowly scrapping the armrest. I've learned that she does this when she is most lucid.

It's another cloudy morning, but warmer than the day before. According to the local weather forecast, temperatures are expected to climb to seventy degrees by this afternoon. Summer is sneaking in. I make a mental note to ask Mr. Caine if Emilia has a wheelchair so I can take her on a nature walk.

"Mrs. Caine?" I slide the book on the coffee table between us. "Do you mind if I borrow your laptop?"

Emilia doesn't move—which isn't a protest.

"Thank you." I rise from the chair and grab the laptop that's been sitting on the dresser since the day I arrived.

I power it up and settle into the chair next to Emilia.

The internet browser opens immediately. No password. I open the search engine and type: *Meredith Nichols, Rock Hill, GA.*

After a few minutes of sleuthing, I learn that Thomas's ex-wife is a Rock Hill native and, as Thomas mentioned, has been married four times. Thomas was her first husband. They married immediately after high school and divorced not long after, as he'd said.

Meredith then remarried at age twenty-four (a trucker named Chuck), then again at thirty (Benny, an auto mechanic). Her latest marriage (John, a shoe salesman) ended three years ago. Her longest marriage lasted eight years.

I click to another page and am shocked to discover that Meredith has a criminal history—an *extensive* history that includes time in county lockup. Over the course of her adult life, Meredith Nichols has had one DWI, a few public intoxes, one indecent exposure, one assault charge. Most recently she was arrested for possession of a controlled substance. According to the article, Meredith had stolen multiple prescription drugs. Pills.

I linger on the assault charge, recalling how she almost slapped me when we first met. My stomach sinks. What if I hadn't woken last night when Meredith went to Emilia's bedroom? Did I avert a devious plan?

I close the browser and replace the laptop on the dresser. I want so badly to ask Emilia about Meredith. To learn more about what appears to be one tangled love triangle.

TWENTY-EIGHT
EMILIA

Then

It was one week after Thomas choked me in the bathroom and blackmailed me when the calls began.

It was 3:07 a.m.

The house was dead silent. Thomas had been locked in his shop for days; we hadn't even spoken. A part of me thought it was because he didn't want to see the bruises on my neck or the claw marks from his nails.

My eyes were bloodshot and dry, fixated on the map spread across the desk. Dots marked potential James sightings—flickers of hope in a sea of despair. My fingers traced the red lines I had drawn, connecting places and people, trying to make sense of it all. The nightmare of his disappearance still felt fresh, despite the many years between then and now. I rubbed my eyes, feeling dizzy from lack of food, of sleep.

My cell phone lit up, startling me.

The flashing number read: *Unknown Caller*.

Unknown Caller? My heart skipped a beat and my hand

shot out, almost of its own accord, to answer the call, as if it knew, deep down, that this was the moment.

I pressed the phone to my ear, my breath shallow, my palms clammy.

"Hello?"

Silence.

My heart hammered against my ribcage. It was him. I knew it was him. "James?" My voice cracked. I surged out of the chair and began pacing. "James? Is that you? James!"

The words stumbled out, desperate.

"Hello?" I repeated, my voice straining against the tightness in my chest. "Is anyone there?"

Tears blurred my vision as the seconds stretched into an eternity. One minute. Two. Three. I kept calling his name, my heart shattering with every passing second.

"Please," I whispered, barely audible through the tears. "Please, talk to me. Please, bring my baby home, please..."

But there was nothing but breathing on the other end of the line.

That was the first call.

The first of countless.

The police told me it was just kids, bored and heartless, playing games at my expense. "Ignore them," they said. As if I could. As if every time the phone rang, my heart didn't lurch with hope and dread, twisting together into something unbearable.

So I waited. Every night, I sat by the phone, staring at it, willing it to ring. I stopped turning off the lights. I stopped eating. I lived in a hollow space between anticipation and terror, fingers hovering over the receiver, wondering if this time, *this time*, it would be different.

But it never was. Some nights, they whispered in the dark, breathing heavy, distorting their voices into cruel imitations.

Other nights, they taunted me. *"I know where he is."* I would beg, plead, promise them anything, but they always hung up.

I knew they were lying. I knew they were feeding off my pain. But what if—what if just once, one of them wasn't? What if I ignored a call that mattered? What if, in my exhaustion, I missed his voice calling for me?

So I stayed awake. I waited. And with every call, I shattered a little more.

TWENTY-NINE
LUCY

Now

The moment Emilia drifts into her afternoon nap, I grab the monitor and clip it to the waistband of the black pants I wear every day.

I need to breathe. The walls of this glass house are closing in on me. The oppressive silence of the second floor, the betrayal and infidelity of the first floor.

Yes, Meredith is still here. And every hour she lingers, my disgust for Mr. Caine grows. I haven't seen him all day, and I can't shake the gnawing thought of what they might be doing.

Keeping one eye on the monitor's reception, so that I don't stray too far out of range, I step outside. My feet crunch against the gravel path as I make my way toward the cliff that overlooks the ravine, where the bench sits that Consuelo told me about. The one Thomas made for Emilia when they first moved here.

I stand at the edge of the cliff, the warm breeze of early spring brushing against my skin, pulling at the edges of my shirt. Below me, the ravine stretches out, with sharp, craggy rocks spearing up from the bottom.

Like everything Mr. Caine makes, the bench is impeccably crafted. The backrest is a delicate weave of crisscrossing wood, curved to support the spine. *Thomas and Emilia Forever* is carved into the armrest, flanked by tiny hearts at each end.

I glance back at Emilia's room, with its sweeping windows reflecting the shifting outdoors. She sits behind one of those panes day after day, and I wonder, is this bench what her eyes linger on? Does she long for the days when her husband truly loved her? When everything was simpler, when trust hadn't been shattered?

A gust of wind stirs the leaves around me, and an unshakable sensation creeps in, as if someone is watching me.

I decide to go back inside, retreating from the vulnerability that comes with the vast wilderness that surrounds the Caine estate.

I'm in the kitchen making Emilia's late-afternoon snack when Consuelo walks in.

I drop the butter knife and spin around. "I am *so* happy you're here."

"I figured you'd be," she deadpans.

"So you know Meredith's here?"

She nods, obviously disapproving, too. Good. We're on the same page.

Consuelo lifts the coffee pot and tops off her travel mug. She looks different today. Her eyes are heavily shaded, her hair frizzed and knotted.

"Thomas texted me last night." Consuelo adds creamer and sugar to the mug.

"He did?"

I wait for her to give me the gossip. She doesn't, but there's no question she's upset about it. Jealousy, perhaps?

Treading lightly, I retell the story of how Meredith almost hit me when I opened the door, and how Mr. Caine averted the attack. Consuelo doesn't seem surprised by this, despite the animated, super-dramatic tone in which I delivered it. I can't help it. I've been dying to talk to someone.

Consuelo's lips press into a thin line. "Meredith is a serious alcoholic—and a serious bitch."

I blink at the emotion behind the words. Definitely jealous.

She continues, "The first time Meredith showed up unannounced was at the old house in Rock Hill." She screws the lid on her coffee mug so tightly her knuckles turn white. "*After* Thomas was married to Emilia."

"How awful for Emilia." *And for you?*

"Yes, but it's not consistent. She's gone long stretches of leaving them alone. The occurrences usually pick up after her divorces."

"How does Emilia deal with it?" I ask.

"Before the stroke... not good. Now, I don't think she even knows."

"Not good, how so?"

Consuelo leans a hip against the counter, glancing at the doorway. "The first two times, Emilia handled it with class. She remained calm, but when Meredith wouldn't leave, she called the cops, waited patiently, and then calmly asked Meredith not to come back. But Thomas would never press charges and it bothered Emilia."

"Of course it did!" I snap. "It's all so messed up!"

"I agree. One time, there was a fight."

"A physical fight?"

"Yes. Meredith caught Emilia on one of her bad days—this was after James disappeared. Emilia lost it and went at her like a rabid dog. I was there. In fact, I broke it up."

"Was anyone hurt?"

"A few scratches, but no. Although, I don't know what would've happened if I hadn't been there."

"What did Mr. Caine do?"

"He drove Meredith home."

I wait for the "and," but it never comes. Instead, Consuelo grabs a granola bar and turns to leave.

"Consuelo, I need to tell you something," I step into her path. "I caught Meredith sneaking into Emilia's room late last night."

"*What?*" The intensity of her response verifies how serious and strange it was.

"I was in my bedroom when I heard her come up the stairs. When I looked out the door, Meredith was standing in the doorway, watching Emilia sleep. It was weird and incredibly creepy, to say the least."

"Did you tell Thomas?"

"No. I never see him. He's always locked away in his shop. Should I?"

"No," Consuelo says quickly. "Let me handle it."

"I'll tell you how it needs to be handled—the woman needs to be kicked out of this house. What if Emilia found out she's here? That her husband allows her to stay the night?"

"She wouldn't be happy about it."

I throw my hands into the air. "Of course she wouldn't! It's ridiculous! I don't understand why Mr. Caine doesn't handle it. What is his *problem?* Why is he like this?"

"You think Thomas just *became* this way?" She shakes her head. "No. Men like him—they are made."

"What do you mean?"

"He grew up *poor,*" she continues. "Very poor. His father—" She makes a sharp gesture with her hand, like cutting through the air. "He was terrible. Strict. Controlling. Always reminding Thomas that their life was fragile, that one wrong move could bring everything crashing down. Thomas used to tell me stories when he was drunk, back when he still thought I was just some housekeeper who would listen and forget."

She exhales slowly, shaking her head. "His father controlled everything. What they ate, what they wore, how they spoke. His mother was barely allowed to leave the house, and when she did, it was only to church or the market, and always under his watch." Her voice lowers. "I don't think she ever loved him, but she was *afraid* of him. And that was enough."

A heavy silence stretches between us before she continues.

"Thomas wasn't allowed to be a child. There was no playing, no dreaming, no nonsense. Just work, discipline, and survival." She tilts her head slightly. "Did you know his father used to lock him in a closet when he misbehaved? Told him, *If you want control, learn how to be still first.*"

Something cold coils in my stomach.

"His mother died when he was a teenager," she says, voice flat. "Thomas was the one who found her. He never talks about it, but I saw it in his face once—guilt. Regret. Maybe even... relief."

I stare at her, the pieces clicking together in my mind. *Control.* That's what Thomas craves, isn't it? Not just over people, but over *everything*—his image, his career, the house, the way the world perceives him. Because he grew up in a world where he had none.

Consuelo leans forward, eyes sharp. "That's why he is the way he is, Lucy. He swore he'd never be powerless again. Never be poor again. Never let anyone else dictate his life." She lets out a humorless chuckle. "But in trying to escape his father, he *became* him."

I swallow hard, gripping the edge of the counter. "Emilia never stood a chance, did she?" I murmur.

Consuelo shakes her head. "No," she whispers. "She didn't."

Her phone blinks, she pulls it from her pocket and taps the screen.

"Dammit, I forgot. The security company is coming soon to fix some of the cameras. I need to transfer some files before they do."

THIRTY
LUCY

Now

It's been weeks and Meredith is *still* here. Mr. Caine's ex-wife is living her best life. Whether she's sleeping in, eating all the food, or coming and going as she pleases, one thing remains constant: she's drunk. The woman *stays* drunk. Morning, noon, and night; drunk.

Meanwhile, the *real* Mrs. Caine is upstairs unable to speak for herself.

I'm ruminating on how messed up this situation is as I step into the master bedroom with Emilia's afternoon snack.

A flash of movement startles me.

Emilia stumbles from the shadows, her arms reaching out, her nightgown stained with coffee. Her movements are jerky and desperate.

I scream, dropping the tray. Tea and water go everywhere. Glass shatters. Utensils clatter against the hardwood.

Emilia is walking on her own! And not just that, she's grabbing for me, clawing the air while wobbling like a rubber doll.

Her eyes are wild, her face contorted. Her body is encased in a murky green-brown glow.

I stumble backward and trip over a pair of shoes.

Her aura. *I can see her aura!*

My backside hits the edge of the bed.

Still grabbing for me, Emilia opens her mouth to say something, but only a thin line of drool drips out.

Just then, Mr. Caine lunges through the doorway. "Emilia!"

A sudden burst of movement fills the room. Meredith is here now, screaming and shouting. Consuelo is hot on her heels.

"*What did you do?*" someone screams at me.

"*What happened?*"

"*Help her!*"

I blink wildly, stunned by not only everything that's happening around me but of the sudden appearance of color in the room. I can see *everyone's* auras. Each merging together in one swirling, violent orb of light. I feel sick, nauseous. It's all too much.

"Consuelo!" Mr. Caine yells. "Get her medicine!"

Consuelo doesn't move. Instead, she's frozen in place, screaming "*Don't hurt her!*" as Mr. Caine wrestles Emilia to the ground. They begin yelling over each other and eventually, Consuelo snaps into action. I stumble out of the way. Emilia is on the floor, mumbling now, drooling, but still grasping for me. The halo around her head grows brighter and brighter.

Consuelo returns from the bathroom seconds later with a syringe in her hand. I watch in horror as Mr. Caine shoves the needle into Emilia's arm.

Together, we watch as Emilia goes limp and her eyes roll back in her head.

Her aura disappears.

Chest heaving, Mr. Caine gapes at me. He's as shocked as I am. "What happened?"

"Nothing." I raise my palms in surrender. "I didn't do anything, I promise."

I drop to my knees and begin gathering the shards of broken glass and clumps of food that cover the floor. My mind is racing, recalling the colors I saw in Emilia's aura.

I've only seen such a stark color twice before. Both clients were suffering severe trauma. One, her child was in the ICU and she was begging me to tell her that he was going to survive. The other was a heroin addict fighting both the craving and the desire to be clean. The murky green color I saw on all three women translates to complete and utter desperation.

My heart hammers as I picture the look on Emilia's face as she grabbed for me.

Desperation.

"Tell me what happened." Mr. Caine barks, pulling me from my thoughts.

"I walked into the room..." My voice is shaking. "And she was standing in the corner."

"She was standing by herself?"

"Yes, over there in the shadows." I gesture over my shoulder.

"And then what?"

"And the second I walked in, she lunged for me."

"No, that can't be right. You're lying. Emilia doesn't walk." This comment comes from Consuelo, who until five minutes ago, I would have called a friend.

"That's what happened," I confirm. "I'm sorry—but that's exactly what happened. I'm not lying."

Mr. Caine shakes his head and returns his focus to his wife.

I look over my shoulder.

Meredith is gone.

THIRTY-ONE
THOMAS

Then

I slid the key into the lock, my fingers trembling slightly as I twisted it. I was nervous, and this surprised me. It was the first time Meredith was going to see the main house, not just the workshop. I wanted her to appreciate the culmination of everything I had worked for. The clean lines, the towering ceilings, the sheer, undeniable success of it all.

"Are you sure Emilia's not here?" Meredith asked, hovering behind me. Her gaze flicked up to the towering glass façade, the sleek modern angles bathed in the afternoon light.

"Yes, I'm certain. I watched her leave this morning before I went into the shop."

"Where did she go?" She stepped closer, her body brushing against mine.

"A doctor's appointment," I turned the knob and pushed open the door. "She finally agreed to see someone about her depression."

Meredith gasped as we stepped inside. "Thomas," she whispered in awe.

I turned toward her, my lips curling into a smile, waiting for praise, for that familiar glow of approval.

As always, my mistress delivered.

"I am so—*so*—proud of you, baby," she said, her voice trembling. "You did this. You really did." She clapped her hands together, giddy. "Show me around!"

Her excitement was infectious. I grabbed her hand, leading her toward the great room.

We froze mid-stride.

Photos were everywhere.

Dozens of them, scattered like fallen leaves across the hardwood floor. Shots of me arriving at the motel where Meredith and I used to meet for our mid-day rendezvous. Shots of Meredith arriving at the new home, while Emilia had *said* she'd gone into town for groceries. The worst of it was the erotic collage in the center of it all. One of us having sex on the motel bed, shot with a long-range camera. Another of her on her knees. The others, various stages of intercourse.

"Oh *shit*." I whispered.

"She knows?" Meredith's voice was barely audible. "Emilia's been following us?"

I didn't answer. I couldn't.

I stepped forward carefully, my heart hammering against my ribcage, and picked up the single sheet of paper at the center of it all. Meredith read over my shoulder as I unfolded it with trembling fingers.

Dear Thomas,

By the time you read this, I'll be gone.

I know how this will play out in your mind. You'll scoff, maybe even laugh, and tell yourself that I'll be back. That I'm weak. That I don't have the courage to leave you.

For years, you've made sure I believed that too.

You built a cage around me, not with chains, but with words. Cutting, insidious words that chipped away at who I was until all that remained was a version of me that fit inside your world. You made me question my own thoughts, my own memories, made me think I was responsible for your endless infidelity. Every time I tried to leave, you pulled me back, not with love, but with fear. The threats, the mind games, the way you always knew just what to say to keep me second-guessing myself.

You called it love.

I call it a pathetic excuse for a man.

I deserved better, and James deserved better.

I'd rather live in hell than another day under your control.

Enjoy the life you've built on manipulation, deceit, and betrayal. I hope it keeps you warm when you're alone with your regrets.

No longer yours,
Emilia

The letter slipped from my hands, fluttering on the air before settling onto the pile of obscene images.

I didn't think. My body just reacted. I spun on my heel and bolted down the hallway.

"Thomas!" Meredith yelled, scrambling after me.

The house felt suddenly suffocating, closing in with every step. My feet pounded against the floor as I threw open the garage door.

Emilia's BMW was still parked inside.

My stomach lurched.

She hadn't left.

"Fuck!" I gasped.

I spun and tore through the house, Meredith's voice a distant echo behind me.

"Emilia!" I bellowed.

No answer.

I took the stairs two at a time, my legs burning, my vision blurring, my pulse a violent drumbeat in my skull.

"Emilia! Emilia!"

I burst into the master bedroom. The bed was made, the lights off.

The bathroom door was ajar, spilling a dim golden glow onto the hardwood floor.

I lunged to push it open.

My world stopped.

The room was dimly lit. The bathtub was full, the water was dark, murky. Emilia lay beneath the surface, her pale arms floating, her white hair fanned out like a ghostly halo.

For a second, my body forgot how to function. I stood there, frozen, as a cold, dead weight crushed my lungs.

Then I was moving, lunging forward, hands plunging into the water, gripping her limp body and dragging her onto the cold tile.

"Emilia!" My voice was raw, guttural.

Water spilled across the floor, soaking my knees, my sleeves. Her skin was like ice. Her lips, a pale blue.

"No, no, no—shit, Emilia. Shit!"

I began CPR, pressing my hands against her chest, pumping, counting, breathing into her mouth.

"Thomas..." Meredith's voice was distant, her steps hesitant.

I didn't stop. I couldn't. I pressed harder, the force of my compressions rocking her fragile frame.

Suddenly, Emilia jerked violently, water spurting from her mouth as she began to cough.

THIRTY-TWO
THOMAS

Then

The doctor closed the door softly behind him as he stepped out of the master bedroom.

I stood beside him, wringing my hands, my stomach twisted into knots.

He took a slow breath before speaking. "Hopefully, now that she's home from the hospital, she'll start to get better. I'm so sorry you have to go through this, Mr. Caine. Attempted suicide weighs heavily on the caregiver as well."

Caregiver. The word made my skin crawl.

"Thank you," I said, my voice hoarse. Then, hesitating, I asked, "So... do people recover from severe anoxic brain injury?"

His expression shifted—just slightly, but I caught it. The momentary hesitation before answering.

"Your wife's brain was deprived of oxygen for more than five minutes, which caused significant damage, killing brain cells and leaving her severely impaired." He cleared his throat. "If you had arrived just minutes later, she wouldn't have survived."

But I did arrive. And now here we are.

"That said," the doctor continued, "I've seen cases where patients improve when they're back home, in familiar surroundings. Sometimes, miracles do happen." He offered a small, almost pitying smile. "I'll pray for that, for you."

I forced a nod, my fingers digging into my palms.

"Is there anything else you need before I go?" he asked.

"Yes, actually." I straightened, forcing control back into my voice. "Can we seal Emilia's medical records? I don't want it getting out that she... that she tried to take her own life."

The doctor nodded reassuringly, as if he had expected the request. "Especially with your notoriety, no, that won't be a problem."

Notoriety. Another word that sat heavy in my gut. I wondered if he was referring to my career or my missing son.

"Thank you."

Once the doctor disappeared down the stairs, I exhaled, pressing my fingers to my temples. The house felt too quiet, too still, the kind of silence that felt suffocating.

Meredith stepped out of the bedroom adjacent to the master suite, where she had been hiding. She stopped beside me, her gaze fixed on the closed door at the end of the hall.

"What are you going to tell people?" she asked quietly.

I stared at the door, at the weight of everything behind it. "That Emilia suffered a stroke. No one will question it after all the stress and trauma of losing James."

Meredith nodded, satisfied.

I turned toward her, my jaw tight. "Can I tell you something?"

"Anything."

"I wish she'd died."

Meredith's lips trembled, tears brimming in her eyes. She swallowed hard before whispering, "Me too. God, Thomas, I do too."

A long moment stretched between us.

"Can I tell you something?" she asked.

I nodded.

"I... might have had a hand in Emilia's unraveling."

"What do you mean?"

Meredith chewed on her bottom lip, her eyes darting to the floor. "I might have... pranked called her a few times."

"What?"

"I know, I know. It's awful." She blew out an exasperated breath. "I just wanted her to *leave*. Leave town, leave you. And so, there were nights when I'd get drunk and I'd call her just to mess with her."

"What would you say?"

"Nothing. She thought it was James calling, or whoever took him."

"Jesus, Meredith." I jabbed my fingers through my hair.

"I know, honey." She grabbed my hands, pulled me to her. "I just hate her so much. You know that. You have to understand. Emilia has put you through so much. For *years*. She's an awful, selfish, manipulative bitch who took the easy way out. She chose suicide for no other reason than to make you suffer."

I felt my pulse spike with anger. How did it come to this?

After a moment, Meredith shifted, glancing at me cautiously. "Thomas... I was thinking... I—I know someone. Someone who can help."

"What do you mean?"

"Pills," she said quickly, her voice barely above a whisper. "Sedatives. I know someone who can get them for us. Enough to keep her... quiet. Comfortable. Unaware."

I stared at my mistress, something dark and twisted coiling in my stomach.

"That way, she's just lying there," she continued. "We won't have to sneak around anymore. No more pretending. And she's just... comfortable."

The silence between us felt different now. Heavier. Like we had stepped past some invisible line, and there was no going back.

I studied Meredith's face, searching for hesitation. There was none.

"Who do you know?" I asked.

"My dealer," she said, meeting my gaze without wavering. "I trust him. I've been buying from him for years."

The house groaned around us, the wind rattling faintly against the windowpanes, as if the very walls knew what was being set into motion.

"Do it," I said, my voice firm. Final.

Meredith exhaled, her lips curling into a small, relieved smile.

"Good for you," she said, gazing up at me. "Good for *us*."

THIRTY-THREE
LUCY

Now

Despite the fact that I was attacked by the woman I've been hired to care for, Mr. Caine did not offer to give me the day off. On the flip-side, I wasn't fired, so I guess I should be grateful.

After the incident, Mr. Caine drugged his wife and retreated to his shop, like always. No hesitation, no remorse—just the same tired routine, as if sedating her was the easiest way to erase the problem. As if she were an inconvenience rather than his *wife*. I try to swallow the frustration constantly burning in my chest, but it's getting harder. Every day, I watch him treat her like an afterthought, a burden he has to manage instead of a woman he once vowed to love.

I'm growing more and more irritated at his blatant disregard. The way he barely looks at Emilia, the way he shuffles her off to sleep instead of trying to engage, trying to *help*. Some days, I get the sinking feeling he doesn't want her to recover at all. That the silence, the distance, is easier for him. She is the one trapped in this fog, lost in a world she can't fully reach, and yet *he's* the one who gets to turn his back and pretend she isn't there.

She deserves better than this—better than being kept sedated and tucked away like a forgotten relic of his past. And the worst part? She can't even fight for herself.

It makes me sick.

I am also rocked by the fact that I can suddenly see auras again. Why now? After so many years? This can only mean one thing: my instincts are heightened. And in my experience, this means something big is about to happen.

There is a heavy air of tension in the home. The glass walls feel like living breathing things, a flection of contorted faces, clowns, taunting me. Warning me. A part of me wants to pack my bag and leave. But I remind myself that I have nowhere to go —literally. And here is better than living in the back of my Tahoe again.

Everyone disappeared downstairs after the incident. No one has asked if *I'm* okay. Everyone in this house is too wrapped up in their own self-loathing world to empathize with those around them. I can't begin to imagine how Emilia feels.

I lean forward, stroking Emilia's forearm, willing her to wake. The drugs Mr. Caine gave Emilia knocked her out for the entire day. I haven't been able to feed her, which bothers me. She needs to drink and eat and I'm the only one who seems to care.

She needs *so much more* than this godforsaken household offers her.

I am fully prepared for whatever might happen when she wakes. I've imagined every scenario possible for when she sees me again, and I've decided that if Emilia wants to use me as a punching bag, I will let her. Because while Thomas translates Emilia's outburst to be something negative, I see it as a huge breakthrough. From what I understand, this is the first time Emilia has shown significant emotion since the stroke. Perhaps this means she's making progress in her recovery. Maybe soon she'll start talking again. The thought fills me with joy. I want that for her. I want her to get better so that she can get up and walk out of this house and divorce her deadbeat husband.

"Emilia?" I whisper gently.

This time, her eyes flutter, but remain closed.

Resigned, I sit back and study her aura. Though dimmed from the sedatives, it's still a dirty, murky green—desperation.

Desperate for what? To get better? To leave her husband? To get out of this house? To find her missing son?

My gaze drifts out the window, to the bench at the edge of the cliff.

Thomas and Emilia Forever.

When I look back at Emilia, her eyes open. She's staring directly at me.

"Oh." I startle, half-expecting her to launch herself out of her chair and lunge for me again.

She doesn't. Instead, we stare at each other, and with each passing second my heart begins to beat faster with an instinct somewhere deep inside.

"Tell me, Emilia," I whisper, leaning in. "Tell me what you're trying to say."

THIRTY-FOUR

LUCY

Now

Meredith stumbles into the kitchen, nearly face-planting as she grabs the doorframe for support.

I don't acknowledge her at first. I keep my focus on the pot in front of me, stirring Emilia's potato soup with slow, deliberate motions. I can already smell the stench of alcohol radiating off her.

"Carbs will make you fat," Meredith slurs, rolling her eyes.

I tighten my grip on the wooden spoon. Of all the things to come out of her mouth, *that's* the first?

Releasing the doorframe, she wobbles into the room, swaying like a top-heavy drunk teetering on the edge of collapse.

I finally turn to face her, my expression flat. She looks like hell. Hair a mess. Makeup smudged. Dress wrinkled. The perfect portrait of a woman who doesn't belong in this house, no matter how much she wants to.

God, I *hate* her.

She notices my stare, nostrils flaring. "Move out of the way."

I don't move.

She squares her shoulders. "I said, *move*."

When I still don't, she grabs my arm, trying to push me aside. I jerk away, the heat rising in my chest before I can stop it.

"Touch me again, Meredith," I seethe, "and I swear to God, I'll break your arm."

"But then how would you wipe Emilia's ass?"

"Better than licking Mr. Caine's."

Her jaw drops. "How dare you!"

I press in, reveling in the emotional release this confrontation is giving me. "How does it feel to be a man's second choice?"

"I am not his second choice." Her lips curl into a sneer. "Look around. Who's living here? Who does Thomas have dinner with every night? Who sleeps in his bed? Who does he spend his time with? *Me!*"

I take a step closer, lowering my voice just enough to make sure she hears every word. "He could throw you out tomorrow, and you'd go right back to the bar to find your fifth—or is it sixth?—husband."

"At least I can *get* a husband," she snaps, jabbing a finger into my chest. "You're pushing forty and still single. No man wants you. And you'd better watch how you speak to me. Soon, you'll be reporting to me. Thomas will put Emilia in a nursing home. Then he'll marry me, and you'll be gone."

"Or he'll get bored of you and find someone else," I say smoothly. "Someone younger. Prettier."

She staggers back like I've slapped her. For a moment, she just stares, her lips parting slightly. Then, aghast, she says, "Are you talking about Consuelo?"

I cock a brow.

She snorts, wobbling slightly. "Please. I took care of that bitch a long time ago."

"You can't even take care of yourself, let alone someone else."

"She's an *illegal immigrant*, you fool. Her boyfriend smuggled her into the country in the trunk of his car. She confided in me one night, thinking we were friends." She snorts. "What a naïve idiot. I threatened to have her deported if she so much as looked at Thomas the wrong way."

I blink, taking a moment to process this new information. "That's why she's so loyal to him," I murmur. "He pays her well and doesn't ask questions."

Meredith waves a dismissive hand. "She's loyal to *me*, not him. She's a whipped dog."

My stomach turns at the way she says it, like she enjoys it, like she relishes the power she holds over someone else.

"You are unbelievable." I shake my head.

"No, I'm *smart*, Lucy. I protect what's mine. *Thomas is mine*, this house will be *mine*—"

I let out a dry laugh. "You mean his *money* will be yours."

"I've *earned* his money." Spittle flies from her lips as she speaks. "I've stood by his side for years. His money is *my* money, and I'll spend every penny before I die."

The baby monitor in my hand crackles to life.

Meredith's head whips toward it. "Uh-oh," she says with mock sympathy. "Looks like Emilia needs her ass wiped again."

"You're such a *bitch*." I turn off the stove and push past her, knocking her aside with my shoulder as I move toward the hall.

Meredith spins, nearly losing her balance, clutching the counter for support. "Don't forget your place in this house, *Lucy Greer!*" she hisses after me. "You're *the help*. Nothing more."

I don't stop or look back. Because I know, without a doubt, that the only real difference between Meredith and me is that she doesn't realize she's being used.

THIRTY-FIVE
LUCY

Now

Later, I find Consuelo in the kitchen, making Thomas another charcuterie board. I step next to her, grab a knife, cutting board, and a handful of fruit. Her gaze flickers to me as we begin working seamlessly together. Though unlike the first time we did this, today her mood is foul.

She's slicing so vigorously that she's broken a sweat. The knit cardigan she usually wears is draped over the bar stool behind her, and her sleeves are rolled up to her elbows. It's speckled with dirt, and I remember seeing her earlier in the garden, tending to plants.

I note that her aura is darker today, riddled with insecurity, worry, and pain—despite her strong, independent exterior.

"How's your day?" I ask.

"Busy. I've been in the garden, and then in the security room, filtering through footage and filing it away, per Mr. Caine." She glances at the clock glowing from the microwave. "In fact, I need to get back up there soon." Her words are harried as if her mind is somewhere else completely.

"Where is the room?"

"It's a small closet adjacent to the media room." Using her forearm, she wipes the sweat from her brow.

"Oh my God." I set down the knife and gape at the nasty, mottled bruise around her bicep.

Consuelo looks at her arm, then quickly grabs the cardigan and slips it on.

"What happened to your arm?" I can't pretend like I didn't see it.

"It's..." she stutters. "I fell."

She's lying. Pitifully. The pattern of bruises is consistent with the mark of a hand, complete with all five fingertips.

"Consuelo." I struggle for words, so I land with: "I'm—I'm here if you need to talk."

To my shock, tears fill her eyes.

"It's not what you think," she mutters.

"I think it's exactly what I think." I close the inches between us. "I've seen this with several of my clients, back in LA, who were seeking advice about their abusive partners." I reach forward and cringe when she flinches. "Who did this to you? Was it your boyfriend?"

Consuelo turns away and braces herself against the sink. A tortured expression squeezes her face—the exact expression she wore when Mr. Caine was pinning Emilia to the ground as Consuelo steamed: *Don't hurt her!*

It hits me then that Consuelo's emotional reaction was triggered because she herself, has experienced abuse.

Suddenly everything makes sense. The ever-vigilant look in her eyes. The tough-girl façade. The constant long sleeves, despite the temperature. The scar down her face.

"Consuelo, you don't have tell me who did it, but we can get you help. *I* can get you help."

"No you can't."

"Well, you're right, actually—I can't help you unless you *talk to me*."

"There's nothing to talk about."

"Your aura tells a very different story."

She turns to me, her watery eyes widening. "You can see my aura?"

"As glaring as that handprint around your bicep."

"What does it say?"

"That you feel hopeless."

Consuelo collapses into sobs. I gently guide her onto the floor, hiding us behind the island in the center. My heart cracks. This outwardly steely woman has hit her breaking point. Everyone has one. I learned that long ago.

"You don't know the circumstances—you wouldn't understand."

"Try me," I say.

"There are things I have to do to survive. Commitments I've made. Mistakes that have trapped me a bit."

"Consuelo, I lived in my car for months before I got this job."

"You did?" She blinks away the tears, surprised.

"Yeah. I was homeless before I started working here. Believe me, I understand surviving, making mistakes, being trapped, and I definitely understand feeling hopeless."

Consuelo studies me for a minute, seeing me in a new light. That's the thing about auras. You don't always have to see them to *see* someone.

"What does my aura look like?"

"Like crap."

She laughs, sucking back the watery mess of her face.

I smile, take her hands gently in mine. "Your normal color is purple. It's a wonderful color to have. It means you're very caring, intuitive, and sensitive—the exact *opposite* of the badass façade you put on every day." I wink. She smiles softly. "But your purple has dimmed. It's cloudy and murky—"

"And hopeless?"

I nod.

"God, I don't know how I got here." She drops her head into her hands. "I used to be strong. Where I grew up you had to be. The moment you showed weakness, that was it. Your life was over. Figuratively, or sometimes literally. They'd prey on you. Prey on the weak."

My gaze shifts to the faded scar on the side of her face.

"I watched good people disappear," she continues, "Neighbors. Friends. My own cousin—nineteen years old—gone one night and never seen again. If you were lucky, they just took your money. If you weren't..." She exhales sharply. "I fought to get out of our neighborhood, of our town. But my brothers and sisters—they're still there. I feel guilty every damn day for escaping and leaving them behind."

"I'm so sorry."

"You can't tell Mr. Caine about this, okay?"

"About your bruise? I promise I won't. But maybe you should. Maybe he could help."

"No."

"Consuelo, he has tons of money. I'm sure he'd be willing to get you the help you need, and maybe even help your family."

"No, Lucy, please stop."

I sigh. "Please tell me what happened."

Consuelo shakes her head and looks away.

Why won't she come clean? Unless the person abusing her *isn't* her boyfriend. My thoughts flash to Meredith, how she almost slapped me. How she has an assault charge. How much she hates Consuelo.

"Fine," I say, resigned. "If you're not going to tell me, you have to speak to someone."

"No. I have it under control. It's—it's complicated."

I feign shock. "No," I gasp, covering my heart with my hand. "*Really?*"

"Stop." She rolls her eyes, another hint of a smile. "I know it's a cliched response."

I pull my phone from my back pocket and click it on. "I'm going to give you my number—"

"No, it's fine—"

"I'll feel better knowing you have it."

We exchange numbers. Consuelo slides her phone back into her pocket. "Again, please don't tell Thomas. I have the next few days off and the bruises will go away by then. He'd fire me if he knew."

"Why do you say that?"

"Because Thomas doesn't want drama from the help, and I've never given that to him. For years, the man has never asked me a personal question. Not a single one. Trust me, he doesn't care, and doesn't want to know."

"He's such an ass. You've dedicated decades to this man, and yet you still don't feel comfortable asking him for help."

She shrugs. "It is what it is. I don't expect you to understand."

"I do understand, on a different level. Mr. Caine has no idea I'm homeless, and here I am, working in this mansion, around all this opulence, acting like it's totally normal and everything is fine." I pause. "Don't let him have that power over you."

"Thomas?"

"Yeah. We're ashamed to show this man who we are. We're embarrassed because he's successful, famous, and handsome. Oprah once said that a woman should never give a man the keys to her self-worth. You don't have to be perfect at your job every day. No one should hold you to those standards—not even Mr. Caine. I think you should talk to him. Ask him for help."

By her expression, I know she won't.

She looks at her watch. "I need to get going."

"Wait." I squeeze her palm. "Whatever is happening outside these walls, please remember, you're never trapped, Consuelo. There is always a way out. There is always an escape."

"I don't see one, Lucy," she whispers back, tears reemerging.

"Look harder. It's there. Tap into the woman who kept going after she got that scar."

Just then, Meredith storms past the kitchen doorway. Together we peer around the kitchen island. A wild, vile expression mars her face. In her hand is a half-drunk bottle of wine.

She doesn't even notice us.

I roll my eyes. "I can't stand that woman—and I can't *believe* Mr. Caine lets her stay here."

"It's temporary," Consuelo says, watching her disappear down the hallway. "It always is."

THIRTY-SIX
THOMAS

Now

The door to my office swings open.

The Dremel slips from my fingers, clattering onto the floor.

"Shit, Meredith!" I spin around on my stool.

Jesus. Her face is flushed, her eyes wild with wine. I've seen this look too many times before—and it's the last thing I need right now.

"Thomas." She juts out her hip and crosses her arms over her chest. "I'm done."

Not this again. I have to force my eyes not to roll back in my head.

Slowly, I slide my safety glasses onto my head and rise from the stool. "No, you're not."

"Yes, I am."

"Meredith, you're drunk. Go take a nap. I need to work."

"Work!" She throws her hands up. "That's all you do! You go into your little shell and completely ignore everything else around you."

If I had a damn nickel...

I reach for her hands. She slaps them away. "I'm leaving."

"No," I say, far too quickly. The desperation in my voice surprises both of us. I clear my throat, but it's too late. Like a shark smelling blood, she's already latched onto my weakness.

Her. Meredith has always been my weakness.

Emboldened now, Meredith closes the space between us.

"I'm leaving, and I'm not coming back until you fire Lucy and put Emilia in that twenty-four-hour home we talked about."

I blink. "Fire Lucy?"

"Yes."

"Why? What happened?"

"She's... I don't like her. There's something off about her. She's so weird with Emilia, and I think she's stealing."

That's a lie. Meredith doesn't think Lucy is stealing, and she couldn't care less how *weird* Lucy is with Emilia (which, for the record, I agree—she is). Meredith simply wants to be the only woman in my life.

We went through this with Consuelo. Meredith gave me hell for months to fire her. I refused because Consuelo was one of the hardest workers I'd ever met. Eventually, Meredith gave up and never mentioned her again.

"I'm not firing Lucy," I say flatly. "You know I have this exhibition coming up. And do you really want me spending *more* time with Emilia? Because that's exactly what would happen."

Meredith's eyes narrow. "Are you threatening me?"

"No. I'm just saying that without Lucy here, I'd have to take care of Emilia myself. More than I already do."

"I don't like her. She's weird. Something's *off* about her."

Translation: Meredith and Lucy must have had some kind of confrontation. I'm sure Lucy said something to piss her off. But I don't have the patience to be dragged into petty gossip and bickering.

"You're too drunk, Meredith. Maybe if you spent less time drinking—"

I don't see it coming.

The slap cracks across my face, sending me stumbling backward. My heel catches on the leg of the stool, and I trip, falling hard onto the floor. The stool topples over, knocking my tools, sending them tumbling across the tile.

I gape up at her, stunned.

I know Meredith's temper. I've been on the receiving end of her sharp tongue, her talent for emotional warfare.

But she's never *touched* me before.

She glares down at me, chest heaving.

"If you're not careful, Thomas," she says, her voice ice-cold, "you're going to lose me forever. I am no man's second choice."

THIRTY-SEVEN

LUCY

Now

It is just after nine in the evening on this crystal-clear, cool night. A full moon hangs low in the sky, washing a silver glow over the mountains.

From my place in the recliner, I stare at Emilia, the outline of her body on the bed hardly visible in the dark room. For hours, I've been anticipating her waking, but she remains asleep.

I sigh, and lean my head against the headrest. I've barely eaten today and my stomach feels like it's caving in on itself.

Quietly, I push off the chair and tiptoe to Emilia's bed. "I'll be right back," I whisper. "I'm going to get a snack."

I make my way downstairs and into the kitchen.

Nothing appeals to me inside the fridge, so I grab a can of cinnamon almonds, likely reserved for the next charcuterie board, and wander into the great room.

Moonlight streams through the windows, pooling on the white monochrome rugs. I run my finger against the soft, buttery leather couch. Stop to marvel at the grandiose fireplace.

What an amazing life Mr. Caine has.

What a horrible life his wife has.

I wander down the hall, studying the frames and plaques that comprise my boss's ego wall.

I stop at a console table. On it sits a silver-framed eight-by-ten photo. It is of Emilia and Mr. Caine on their wedding day. In it, Emilia's eyes twinkle. Her cheeks are rosy, her smile is beaming.

She looks beautiful.

Movement outside catches my attention. I move to the window and see Consuelo crossing the driveway. Frowning, I watch as she heaves two cans of gasoline into the back of her trunk. I recognize them as the ones Thomas keeps in the garage.

I recall her saying she forgets to fill up at the gas station and often uses Thomas's to top off. But why is she loading the cans into the back of her car? I make a mental note to ask her about it when she returns after the weekend.

Shrugging it off, I turn away from the window and wander back upstairs to Emilia.

THIRTY-EIGHT

LUCY

Now

I make my way up the staircase, glancing out the windows as I pass. My reflection looks distorted in the glass. It reminds me of that famous painting, *The Scream*, by Edvard Munch. Sometimes I feel like I want to grab my face, just like that, and scream, too.

The security lights wash the tree line in a dull orange glow. Beyond it, pitch blackness.

Suddenly, I hear footsteps in the far side of the house. Curious, I turn, hurry down, and hide behind the staircase. Thomas comes into the foyer, casts his eyes around, then turns back down the hallway. Looking for Meredith? It's then that I realize I haven't seen her since our argument in the kitchen.

Where is she?

Something flutters in my stomach. A weird, sixth sense.

Despite the warning bell in my head, I tiptoe down the hall after him.

The door to the guest room where Meredith stores her things is closed. It's never closed.

Thomas, his back to me, knocks lightly and calls her name.

My pulse has already increased when Thomas pushes open the door—and gasps.

I break out into a jog.

Meredith is lying on the bed. Her head is propped up on a pillow, her curly blonde hair fanned out like one big spiderweb. Her eyes are open, staring lifelessly at the doorway, almost exactly where I'm standing. Dried vomit runs from her mouth and down her neck. The front of her shirt is covered in brown chunks.

"Meredith!" Thomas lurches to her bedside. "Oh my God," he chokes out, pressing his fingers against her carotid artery.

I rush into the room, taking in the scene.

On the bed lays an empty bottle of wine. Clutched in Meredith's hand is a brown pill bottle. Three words on the label jump out at me like blinking lights—

Xanax

Emilia Caine

"Oh—*fuck.*" Thomas, unaware of my presence, grabs his head. "Fuck, fuck, fuck!"

What is happening?

I recall how I taunted her during our argument in the kitchen: *"How does it feel to be a man's second choice?"*

Did she do this?

Oh my God, she did it. In a drunken haze of anger and jealousy, Thomas's mistress killed herself using his wife's prescription. The ultimate screw-you to her boyfriend who wouldn't let go of his wife.

Howling, Thomas crumbles to the floor, slamming his closed fists against his temples over and over again.

"Damn you!" he screams. "*Damn you, Emilia!*"

THIRTY-NINE
THOMAS

Now

Twenty minutes later, I'm sitting at the kitchen table, feeling like I am about to vomit.

It is all too familiar. The dark night, the officers in the kitchen, the strangers in the house. The questions—the *damn questions*. Everything reminds me of the night James went missing so long ago. Why does it feel like everything is happening all over again?

After calling 911, Lucy left me and ran upstairs to sit with Emilia until the cops arrived. Now, however, she is pacing a hole in front of the kitchen sink. Twenty years ago, Emilia was sitting at the table, like I am now. She was being interviewed, while I was pacing by the sink. Like Lucy is now.

What a mind-fuck.

Both Lucy and I have given our statements to an officer called Smith, while the other responding officer disappeared to the room where Meredith's body lies. And like when James went missing, I have been asked to stay in the kitchen.

I catch a glimpse of a black body bag being carried into the house seconds before a man steps into the kitchen. He is tall and tanned, with broad shoulders under a deputy sheriff's uniform.

My stomach drops in recognition.

"Mr. Caine," the deputy says, his voice deep and gritty.

"You're—"

"Ryan Perez." He nods. "I worked your son's missing person case years ago. I wondered if you'd recognize me."

I blink, words catching in my throat.

Perez, once a kid, now a full-grown man, gestures to his uniform. "I work for the county police now. After Chief Bobby retired, I moved on."

"Yes, I can see that." I stand shakily. We clasp hands. "Good to see you again—wow, I can't believe it."

"I know. When I heard your name, I gotta admit, it brought up memories. So..." He glances at Lucy. "What's going on?"

"Oh. Sorry." I clear my throat. "This is Lucy Greer. She works for me as a live-in caregiver."

Perez introduces himself to Lucy. They shake hands.

"Tell me about tonight." He returns his focus to me.

I suck in a shuddering breath. "I—my ex-wife, Meredith, is... well, she's dead. I walked into the guest room, where she's temporarily staying, and found her..." I lay a hand on my churning stomach. "With a bottle of pills next to her."

Perez flinches. "Damn, I'm sorry."

I nod, swallowing deeply.

"What kind of pills?" he asks.

"Xanax."

"Hers?"

"No. The prescription belongs to my wife, Emilia."

Lucy has stopped pacing and is listening intently.

"Where is Mrs. Caine now?" Perez asks.

"Upstairs, asleep. She's mostly confined to bed. It's why I hired Lucy."

"I heard about what happened. Awful thing, it is." He pauses to offer a pitied, pained expression. "A stroke, right?"

The knot in my throat tightens. "That's right," I lie.

"Brutal. My grandmother had one a few years ago. I'm so sorry. So, hang on..." Perez scratches the top of his head, once thick with black hair, now thinning. "Help me understand... why is Meredith, your ex-wife, here in the first place?"

I launch into the story of Meredith's random drunken visits. How, when she shows up, she is usually at the end of her rope, and how I care for her until she's back on her feet. I request he search the Rock Hill police records, in case he needs to verify my story.

Perez nods. "I remember she was pretty hung up on you, even during all her marriages. Three, or four, was it?"

I'm reminded of the only reason I agreed to leave Rock Hill. The gossip.

"Did she come here before her last attempt?" he asks.

"Last attempt?" I blink. "What last attempt?"

"Her last suicide attempt." Perez frowns. "This isn't her first. I... I figured you knew."

My back straightens. "What? She tried to kill herself before?"

Perez nods, but his brow remains creased. He doesn't believe that I don't know this. Hell, neither do I.

"She swallowed a bunch of pills after her last divorce. Exact same scenario, except it wasn't Xanax. I was still working for the Rock Hill police then. She barely survived."

I'm utterly shocked. I had no idea. She never told me this.

"How did she get the pills tonight?" he asks.

Lucy speaks. "They're missing from Emilia's medicine cabinet. I checked a few minutes ago. She must have snuck up and got them at some point."

Perez scratches his chin. "So, Meredith's been crashing

here, and now she's dead. Assuming it's suicide, help me understand why she felt like she needed to end her life."

"I don't know."

"Was there an argument between you two?"

I am rendered speechless by another flashback. This one of me being asked this very question about James, the day he went missing.

My lie is the same. "No."

Perez shifts his focus to Lucy. "How about you? Any heated conversations?"

"No." I get the sense she's also lying.

"So, if neither of you triggered it, someone or something else did. What about Mrs. Caine? Have they spoken? If I recall, they had a heated exchange a time or two in the past."

"No. Emilia doesn't speak and also, Meredith is not allowed in my wife's room."

"But... she got the pills, right? So she must've gone in the room at least once."

Fair point.

He continues, "Has anyone else been in the house today?"

"Yes. My housekeeper, Consuelo."

"Consuelo? Wow—Consuelo Sanchez? She *still* works for you?"

"Yes. It's been a long time."

"No kidding." He snorts. "She was here today?"

"Yes, I think so. I can verify on her sign-in log."

"Did she say anything about Meredith? Notice anything off?"

He asks this to both Lucy and me. We both shake our heads.

"Do you have Consuelo's number and address? I'd like to visit her, or give her a call. Get her thoughts on this. She's been around a long time. She's dealt with Meredith before right?"

I'm not sure where he's going with this. Regardless, Perez

jots down the information as I read her phone number and address off my phone.

Our attention is pulled to another stranger entering my home unannounced.

"That's the ME," Perez says.

"The medical examiner?"

Perez nods. "It's procedure. The ME will be the one to officially determine cause of death."

"It was an overdose suicide," I say, far too quickly.

"Yes, I know. I believe you. But we have protocols in place to ensure nothing is missed. For example, if she overdosed, was it accidental or intentional? She loved her pills, everyone knows that. It might not be suicide at all—the tox report will confirm that. Anyway, I'm going to chat with him. I'll be back in a minute."

"Wait, so, what's the process here?" I ask. "I mean, doesn't someone need to call her next of kin or something?"

"As far as I know, Meredith is currently unmarried and she never had kids, right?"

"Right—I mean I don't think so."

Perez nods. "We'll see who she listed as her emergency contact on her medical records. As for the process? The ME will conduct his initial investigation here in the house. Then, we'll bag up the body and take it to the morgue. There, he'll run a toxicology scan on her, and if he feels like there needs to be an autopsy too, he'll do that." Perez shrugs. "Then, once the death certificate is completed, it's up to whoever is listed as her contact on her medical records to deal with the body and funeral, should there be one."

Why do I have a sick feeling that person is me?

FORTY

LUCY

Now

I pivot, pacing Emilia's bathroom with my phone pressed to my ear.

"Come on, come on, *answer*."

I disconnect, then dial for the third time.

"Hello?" Consuelo's scratchy voice sounds through the phone.

"It's Lucy. Sorry for waking you."

"It's two in the morning. Is everything okay?"

"No. I wanted to give you a heads-up: the cops are on their way to question you. Or they might call, I'm not sure."

"*What?*" The sheets rustle as Consuelo shimmies out of bed.

"Meredith is dead. Thomas found her in the guest bedroom. It looks like a suicide. She had Emilia's pills in her hand and an empty bottle next to her."

The pause on the other end of the line is long enough that I check to make sure the call is still connected.

"Why do they want to talk to me?"

"Because you worked earlier today. They have questions for you."

"But I was outside most of the day, doing yard work in the garden. I don't know what I could tell them."

"What about the security footage. Didn't you say you were doing something with that? Was there something on there that recorded Meredith's final moments?"

She hesitates. "I don't look at the videos, I just upload them to the cloud. I don't *want* to look at them."

"Well maybe someone should look at them. You said the room is adjacent to the media room, right? I'll go—"

"No, Lucy. And besides everything is password protected and the door is locked."

"So bring me the key."

"I'm not driving there in the middle of the night to give you the key. You don't need to be going through Thomas's stuff anyway."

"Fine." I begin chewing on my cuticle, my stomach twisting as it has been since I decided to make this call. "Consuelo..."

"Yeah?"

"I need to ask you something."

"What?"

I glance at the closed bathroom door, then, "Did you have anything to do with it?"

"*What?*" she whisper-hisses back.

"Listen, I know Meredith has threatened to turn you in to immigration. Meredith told me everything."

"Where are you going with this?"

"Did you have anything to do with it?"

"Why would you ask that?"

"Because in addition to everything I just told you, I know that Meredith is aggressive, and I know that you two hate each other, and I know that you recently showed up with bruises on your arm—and now she's dead. That's a lot of coincidences."

"You think the bruise on my arm is from Meredith?"

"I don't know what to think!" I hiss back.

"*Lucy*," she says incredulously, "I can't believe—"

"Listen, we don't have time to play games. I'll help you; you just have to tell me."

"I didn't freaking kill her, my *God*."

"*Really?*"

"Really. Geez. If I was going to kill her, I would have done it a long time ago. Probably right after she threatened to have me deported. Trust me on this."

"Where did you get the bruise, then?"

"From my boyfriend, okay?" She snaps. "It was his hand-print on my arm."

"Oh..." I exhale. "That's what I thought initially, but now, with this, I wasn't sure." I scrub my hand over my eyes. "I'm so sorry. Is that where you got the scar on your cheek, too?"

"No, that happened in Mexico when I was a little girl. I stood up to a pandillero for trying to steal my backpack. I got punished for it. Violence has been a part of my life since I was born."

"It doesn't have to be. How long has this been going on?"

"Since forever. But it's not all the time. It ramps up when he's stressed."

"Why don't you leave him, Consuelo?"

"Marcus and I have been together, on and off, since high school. He's the one who got me out of my neighborhood. He's the one who got me to the States. He risked everything bringing me here."

I recall Meredith's words: *Her boyfriend smuggled her into the country, in the trunk of his car.*

She continues. "Remember when I told you I had commitments?"

"Yeah."

"Well, Marcus was a coyote."

"What's a coyote?"

"It's slang for people who smuggle migrants into the US."

"He's a human trafficker?"

"No. Very different. It's an underground network of people who sneak immigrants across borders for big money. I helped him a few times, and I made a promise to my brothers and sisters that we would bring them to the US. But the plans kept falling through—for years. We tried to go the legal route after, but the laws change so frequently and the process is ridiculously long and more expensive than any of us had money for. Also, two of my brothers have rap sheets. It was stressful and we began getting into arguments about it all. Eventually, they said they didn't even want to come." She swallows deeply. "Anyway, I know now that Marcus was promising to help my family just so that I'd stay with him. And I did because I loved him, I felt trapped for having helped him, and also because I had made a commitment to my family."

"So because he did you a favor, and said he'd do the same for your family, that makes it okay for him knock you around? You are *not* indebted to this man, Consuelo. Nor are you to Mr. Caine. We'll figure it out. Let me come get you."

Just then Emilia's movement monitor goes off. I rush to the door and peek into the bedroom, where Emilia is moving gently under the covers.

"Emilia's waking up. I don't want her to—"

"Go. I'm fine."

"Are you sure?"

"Yes. When will you be back?"

"Not for a few days. I've got some time booked off. Going on a road trip to the hiking trials up north."

I recall her taking Thomas's gas cans. Maybe that's why?

"Keep me updated," she says.

"I will."

FORTY-ONE
THOMAS

Now

It's been four days since Meredith died. The toxicology report confirmed suicide—a lethal combination of Xanax and alcohol. Like Emilia's attempt, but this time successful. Of course Meredith would go out dramatically. She did everything that way.

I think of how different she was from Emilia—desperate where Emilia was independent, clinging where Emilia pulled away. After James left, Emilia retreated into herself, making James her sole focus. I became nothing but a chore.

I can't wrap my head around what my life has become. James, Emilia, now Meredith—each loss hollowing me out a little more. But this time, I feel nothing at all. Just numb.

As I mindlessly stroll the halls of this beautiful home I built, I feel absent in my own life. A shell of a human. Lost and aimless.

I find myself at the top of the staircase. The clock on the wall reads one-thirty in the morning. Emilia's door is shut, as it is most days.

I stare listlessly at the closed door, memories of the first time I met Emilia awakening in the corners of my memory. Life before she cheated on me, before James was born and our lives were flipped upside down.

James.

I pivot and make my way to the room Emilia called her "office," when it was really a command center for her never-ending search for James.

A shudder ripples through me as I step inside. I hate this room. It represents the catalyst of sadness in our lives, of every monumental shift in my marriage. I have only set foot in this room three times. Emilia, on the other hand, lived here until her attempted suicide.

The hair on the back of my neck prickles as I journey deeper inside.

Emilia was obsessed with finding James. It literally drove her mad.

My stomach twists as I look down at the mess strewn over the desk. Maps dotted with coordinates of possible sightings, phone numbers, pictures, newspaper articles, CCTV still shots, scribbled notes, dates, times. My head spins.

I pick up a crumpled Post-it.

Gold Loans: Contacted 4/09, again 4/10, 4/13, 4/14. Possible sighting, same height, age, hair color. No compass. Spoke with Eddie and Lisa.

I remember the night of Emilia's breakdown at the pawn shop like the back of my hand. Emilia was certain of two things: One, that James was not kidnapped, and therefore, he ran away. And two, that James would pawn the gold compass I'd once gifted him, because he would need money to survive. Aside from his car, it was the only thing of value he owned that wasn't in the house after he left. Emilia was so stuck on this that she called every pawn shop in the tri-state area. Hundreds of pawn shops knew my son's name, likeness, car. Every sordid detail of his disappearance.

Emilia fixated on a place called Gold Loans, past the state line. They'd reported seeing a vehicle that resembled James's, and also someone who looked like him. Though neither were caught on camera, and therefore, couldn't be proven. But Emilia couldn't let it go. To the point they threatened to charge her with harassment.

I'll never forget walking into the pawn shop, seeing the woman I'd married on the floor, hugging her knees to her chest, rocking back and forth, crying like a baby.

Before I can stop myself, I pull my cell phone from my pocket and dial the number.

"Gold Loans. This is Earl, how can I help you?"

"H... hi." I clear my throat—what the hell am I doing? "This is Thomas Caine."

"Thomas? Holy smokes, it's been a while." Earl's thick southern accent triggers deep, dark memories. "How are ya?"

"Good, uh, fine. I didn't expect to get you."

"Ah hell, I'll die here. I've been working overnight lately. Wife hurt her back, you know how that goes."

I sure do.

"Anyway, I hear you've got some big knife showing coming up."

"An exhibition, yes."

"Man, that's great. Good for you. You still drawing war scenes on the blades?"

"Etching, but yeah. Something like that."

"Etching, yeah, sorry; don't know the lingo. How's the wife?"

"She's hanging in there."

A pause, then, "Good. I'm glad she got the help she needed."

"So, um," I say quickly, "I was wondering if you guys ever came across that gold compass?"

"No, man, sorry. We've had a few that were pawned but none with the name *James Caine* engraved in the center."

I swallow the knot in my throat. "Okay, thanks."

"Any news on that front? Gosh, it's been, what? Twenty years?"

"Around there. And no—no news. Just felt compelled to call."

"Alright, well, I've got your number. As always, I'll let you know if I see anything."

"Thanks."

I disconnect and instantly regret the call.

Sick to my stomach, I close the door and make my way back down the hall, pausing once again at the staircase.

Why *is* the door to the master bedroom always shut? Why has Lucy started doing that?

Careful to avoid the creaking planks, I tiptoe down the hall.

I press my ear to the door. When I hear nothing, I quietly turn the knob and push it open.

I peek inside.

Lucy is asleep, curled next to Emilia.

My gaze narrows. That's weird, right?

Something about this woman is strange. I've felt it from the moment I opened the door and saw her two different-colored eyes.

I think it's time to address it.

FORTY-TWO

LUCY

Now

I press the phone to my ear and turn away from Emilia, who is asleep in the armchair.

"You okay?"

"Yeah. Just not feeling great." The reception crackles, causing Consuelo's voice to break up.

I frown into the bay window that overlooks the ravine. Dusk has settled in the mountains.

"I think I have a cold or something," she continues.

After Consuelo took her scheduled time off, she's called in sick. I don't believe she's actually sick. Something is definitely going on. Not only with her, but Thomas as well. He's been visiting the second floor more frequently than ever before, and I caught him lingering outside my room once. Snooping? I don't know.

"Have the cops called you again?" I ask, needling for details. Mr. Caine has offered little information about what happened that night, and there's nothing on the internet.

"No, thank God." A door opens and shuts as Consuelo steps outside wherever she is. "Anything new there?"

"No. Mr. Caine has closed himself off in his shop," I scoff.

"Do you think Emilia knows Meredith died?"

"No. I don't see how she would. I've been very careful to keep the door shut, and I never leave Mr. Caine alone with her."

"I don't think he'd tell her."

"I wouldn't put anything past him."

"That feels like a loaded statement."

"I just think everyone is beginning to see Mr. Caine in a new light."

"Everyone, who?"

"The cops, mainly. They came by again to ask more questions about Meredith's death. I think they've picked up on the fact that he's an absentee husband and caregiver. Basically that he's a horrible human being."

"Wait... are you saying—do they suspect he had any part in Meredith's death?"

"I don't know. It was officially ruled a suicide, but I'm sure they could re-open the case or something."

"Do *you* think he had something to do with it?"

"I don't know."

"But you know *I* didn't have anything to do with it, right?"

"I know," I lie. The truth is, between Consuelo and Mr. Caine, I don't know what I think. I have a nagging feeling that Meredith wouldn't end her life like that. She was too cocky. Too certain of her and Mr. Caine's future. She'd put up with him for decades. Why end it now?

"What did they do with her body?" Consuelo asks.

"I didn't tell you? Apparently, she'd put Mr. Caine as her next of kin. He's had to deal with everything. The only reason I know is because I overheard him on the phone with the funeral home who had her body."

"Wow, she was *so* obsessed. What did he do with her?"

"Cremated her."

"She would've hated that."

I snort, despite myself. "I know. She probably wanted to be buried in a bejeweled casket."

"Is he doing a funeral?"

"If he's been planning something, I don't know about it."

We sit in silence a moment.

"So," I ask. "When are you coming back?"

"I don't know if I will. Honestly? I'm thinking about quitting and leaving town. Just packing up and getting out of here. Like you did when you left Los Angeles—taking off, drive east, work odd jobs until I can find a stable housekeeping position that I enjoy, and can start over."

"So, does this mean you're considering leaving your boyfriend, then?"

"Leaving everything."

I pause. "I'm proud of you, Consuelo..."

"Thanks, but why do I feel like there's a 'but' coming?"

"Why don't you hang on a few more days?"

"What do you mean?"

"Don't quit. And don't leave yet."

"Why?"

"I have a weird feeling things are going to change around here very soon."

FORTY-THREE
THOMAS

Now

"Hey, Lucy..." I rap my knuckles on Emilia's closed door. It's nine in the morning, and I realize I have no idea when Lucy wakes for the day.

I hear the *pat, pat, pat* of hurried footsteps. The door opens.

Lucy's brown hair is stringy and tangled, and looks oily. I wonder when she showered last. Her eyes are red and puffy, as if she just woke up. Emilia is seated in her favorite armchair, staring out the window. An open book sits on the coffee table.

Lucy remains in the doorway like a blockade.

I force a smile. It's gotten painfully awkward between us.

"Hey, Lucy. Sorry to interrupt. Two quick things: One, I might need you to take on some more duties with Consuelo taking time off. What do you think?"

"That's fine with me, just let me know and I'll do it. What's two?" she asks impatiently. It bothers me. Do I need to remind her that she's in my house, and that I'm her boss? Therefore, she should be clinging onto my every word, eager to please me? Besides, what does she have going that's so important?

Again, I force a friendly smile but it probably looks manic. "Do you remember when you asked if Emilia had a wheelchair, so that you could take her outside on a walk? Get some fresh air?"

Lucy nods.

"Sorry it took me a while, but I remembered I do, in fact, have a wheelchair in the garage. I cleaned it up. It's at the bottom of the staircase." I gesture to the window. "It's a beautiful morning. I thought you could take her out before the storms roll in this afternoon."

Lucy considers Emilia as if silently consulting with her, then turns back to me. "Yes. That sounds good."

"Great," I say, far too quickly. "I'll carry her down now."

"Now?"

"Yeah, why not?"

"O—oh, okay."

I shoulder past Lucy and breeze into the room. It smells different than I remember. It doesn't smell like Emilia anymore. It smells like Lucy.

"Hey, Emilia," I say, suddenly feeling like I'm speaking to a stranger. "Lucy is going to take you outside for some fresh air. I've got your wheelchair cleaned up. Doesn't that sound nice? I'm going to carry you downstairs. Hang onto me tightly, like we've done before. You ready?"

I can feel Lucy's judgment as I clumsily scoop Emilia into my arms. My legs wobble as my thigh muscles ignite.

Lucy follows like a dog as I carefully carry Emilia down the staircase, pretending that I don't feel like I'm about to die.

I practically drop my wife into the wheelchair.

Lucy shoots me a sharp look.

"Okay." I suck in a breath. "The driveway is paved, so that might be the easiest route, but you could also take her to the bench that overlooks the cliff. She loves it there."

Lucy nods and positions herself behind the chair, all but muscling me out of the way.

"Okay then." I smile widely. "Have fun."

FORTY-FOUR

THOMAS

Now

The moment the front door closes, I sprint back upstairs.

Something isn't right with Lucy. I feel it in my gut. Recently, I've realized that I've felt that way ever since I first laid eyes on her. But I pushed aside the red flags because my only concern then was getting Emilia out of my hair.

After a quick peek over my shoulder, I slip into Lucy's room, next to the master bedroom. I close the door behind me.

I'm not sure what I'm looking for, exactly, but I can't resist the urge to learn more about this mysterious woman.

Okay, what first?

Bathroom. All women's secrets are concealed in the bathroom. Everyone knows this.

I go through the vanity drawers first. Makeup, toothbrush, toothpaste, drugstore face cream, a brush, about a million hair ties, pack of gum, and a bottle of Tylenol. Next drawer: Spectacle cleaner, contact solution, a small screwdriver set. Tucked in the back of this drawer is a box of brown hair dye. Probably to cover the beginning of gray hairs, I muse, and then stop to wonder why Lucy isn't married. And presumably, no children. That's odd for an almost-forty-year-old woman, isn't it?

The shower contains a bottle of two-in-one shampoo and a single bar of soap. Irish Spring. The smell reminds me of my father. He used the same brand.

The remaining drawers and cabinets in the bathroom are empty. No feminine products, I note.

...Huh.

I return to the bedroom.

A duffel sits on the floor next to the bed. I almost gag from the scent that wafts out. A worn pair of running shoes are tucked inside, next to an open pack of beef jerky. Candy wrappers and empty bags of chips fill the rest of the space.

Tucked in the bottom is a large, brown folder. Inside is a handful of loose papers and a sketch pad. The faded scent of paint fills my nose. I lift one of the papers. My eyebrows pop. It's a replica of Vincent Van Gogh's famous *Starry Night* painting. An amateur replica, but decent nonetheless. Seven more Van Gogh replicas are scattered among works in progress, in various stages of completion.

Lucy paints? I would have never guessed that. Not in a million years. Feels odd that this didn't come up in our initial conversation.

Something tickles the fringes of my memory but I can't place it.

I quickly replace the paintings and sketch pad and zip up the duffel.

I check the nightstand drawers—empty.

Under the bed—empty.

The dresser—empty.

I hurry to the closet and turn on the light.

In addition to the white shirt and black slacks she wears around the house, three short-sleeve, and three long-sleeve line the shelves—all Hanes, the kind you buy in the pack. Two pairs of jeans are folded on a shelf, next to a half dozen mismatched socks and underwear.

I frown.

Using the tips of my fingers, I pick up a pair of blue underwear.

Underwear, as in boxer briefs—not panties.

The hair on the back of my neck prickles.

I replace the underwear and search for a bra or a sports bra.

I find none.

My pulse begins to race.

I push to my tiptoes and feel around on the shelf that encircles the top of the closet. Nothing, nothing, nothing, until my fingers graze against something hard. But I can't reach it.

Heart drumming, I spin on my heel, run out of the room, and grab a stool from the media room.

My knees feel weak as I step onto the stool. I find the object once again. With it clutched in my hand, I dismount and open my palm.

My stomach drops to the floor.

It is a small, gold compass.

Engraved in the middle is the name:

James Caine

FORTY-FIVE
THOMAS

Now

Lightning flashes outside the window, followed by a bellow of thunder.

Lucy steps into the kitchen and startles when she sees me.

The room is dark, save for a dim yellow light above the stove. I haven't turned on the overhead lights because I have been sitting in this exact spot, in this exact chair, for three hours waiting for my stepson to come downstairs.

He stops. His eyes grow wide at my expression.

Tension crackles between us.

He knows I know.

Even through the darkness, I can see it clearly now. The sharp line of his jaw, the round lips, the crooked right incisor, the nose that's a bit too large for his face. Why didn't I notice the resemblance before? His natural white-blond hair has grown long and been dyed brown. His natural eye color has been changed with two different-colored contact lenses. And a pair of thick, black glasses on top of that.

My stomach folds in on itself.

I flick the compass that's been sitting in front of me for three hours to the center of the table.

James stares at it. His face goes pale.

I can't speak. I want to. I've been sitting here planning a million ways to start the conversation. A million ways to ask the million questions rolling around in my head. But... I. Can't. Speak.

A solid minute passes as we stare at each other.

More thunder in the distance.

"I... I don't know what to say." Her—*his*—voice is now two octaves deeper.

Holy *shit*.

James blows out a breath, resigned to the fact he's been caught. He walks to the sink, takes off his glasses, and splashes cold water on his face.

I watch in awe—Emilia's son, my stepson, is back.

James wipes his face with a towel, smearing the mascara and lipstick he'd applied that morning.

"Why?" It's the only word I can muster.

James snorts as he tosses the towel back on the rack. "How many hours you got, *Dad*?"

FORTY-SIX

JAMES

Now

For five minutes, we say nothing, sitting across from each other at the table.

Not a single word. Just silence stretching between us, thick as the storm raging outside.

I twirl the old compass between my fingers. It feels heavier than it should, like it carries all the weight of the past with it.

I won't look at him. I can't.

"Can we start with what happened the day you disappeared?" Thomas asks, finally.

"I ran away."

There it is. The truth, spoken out loud. My mother was right all along. I was never kidnapped. I wasn't dead. And that truth, no matter how justified my reasons were, sits like a stone in my gut. She mourned me. She grieved for me. And I let her believe it.

"Why, James?"

"Many reasons." I roll the compass over my knuckles, my voice steady, but I feel the old resentment bubbling up like bile.

"Because you hated me. Because you never considered me your son. And worse, you held it over Mom's head. Because you threatened me—and *her*. And because you killed Eugene, my real father."

"I didn't—"

"Yes, you did," I snap, years of anger and pain rushing to the surface. "You can deny it all you want, but I *know* you did."

Thomas leans back slightly, his face unreadable. "Do you have proof of this?"

"I don't need proof. I *saw* your aura that day." I finally look at him, and for the first time, his expression flickers with something—doubt, unease, maybe even fear. "Do you remember the story I told you when I first came here as Lucy? About my ability to see people's auras? It's all true. The day you told me my birth dad died, your aura gave you away. You were lying, scared, and guilty as *hell*. It circled around your head like a poisonous smoke."

"That's not enough to take to the cops."

"I'm not taking it to the cops, you asshole. You'd never get charged. I know that. And unlike you, I care about the ramifications of my decisions. His family—*my* blood—have been through enough."

Despite the sweeping windows and the table between us, the room suddenly feels smaller, like the walls are pressing in. I tighten my grip on the compass, grounding myself.

"Do you remember when I left?" I ask.

Thomas's jaw ticks. He remembers. I know he does.

The night before I ran, I found out about his latest affair—a stupid, careless tryst with a local waitress. Cheri was her name. She had slipped the details to her manager, and within twenty-four hours, the entire town of Rock Hill was buzzing about it.

When I confronted him, I told him I hated him. It was the second time I'd ever said it. The first was when I knew he killed my birth father.

"That night," I continue, "I accused you of murder again, and again, you told me I'd regret saying that. Again, you implied you would *hurt* Mom. And then..." I swallow hard. "Do you remember what you called me?"

He looks away.

"You called me a *faggot*."

Silence.

Eventually, he says: "Do you want me to say I'm sorry? Is that what this is about?"

"I don't need your apologies anymore. But you should know something—I'm not gay, Thomas." I lean forward, forcing him to meet my eyes. "I'm just *different*. I've always been different. And I've felt lost because of it. I'm not a macho, alpha womanizer like you. I don't like sports or hunting or making knives." I pause. "Instead, I see auras. That's my gift. That's why I started painting when I was young. I was too scared to tell you or Mom about it. So I *painted* what I saw. I had to release it somehow. You hated it because it wasn't masculine. And yet, you never even knew *why* I was doing it."

He doesn't respond.

"Everything I told you when I showed up here is true. I moved to LA, changed my name, started a business." I pull off my glasses, setting them on the table between us. "The different-colored eyes and glasses are fake. People like *weirdness* in LA, they gravitate toward it. And they trust female psychics more than male. So I embraced it. I became Lucy, and through her, I no longer had to hide. I became the artist that James was always too scared to be. And it paid the bills for a long time."

Eyes narrowed, Thomas leans forward, elbows on the table. "Why are you here now, James?"

I could give him the easy answer—the one he expects. But I don't. I won't give him the satisfaction of knowing that the main reason for returning was to atone for my mistakes. To finally rid myself of the guilt I've felt for so long. To ask for forgiveness from the only person who was ever there for me. My mother.

"Why did I come here, twenty years later?" I watch his expression. "Because I'm *broke*, Thomas. I lost my business, got evicted, moved into my Tahoe. I decided to leave LA, and I didn't know what else to do."

I look down at the compass, running my thumb over the worn gold surface. "But you should know something. I could *never* let go of this. No matter how much I hated you, I could never bring myself to sell it. For better or worse, you were the father figure in my life."

His expression shifts, just slightly, but I catch it.

"When you got famous, I started following you. I'd scroll through your social media every week. I'd Google you. I'd read the local newspaper online just to see what was going on back home." I pause. "That's how I found the help-wanted ad for this address. I applied just to see what would happen. Honestly, I thought you'd recognize me immediately. I even prepared a speech."

Thomas rubs a hand over his face, exhaling. "James, when you left twenty years ago, you had short white hair and brown eyes. Now, you're an adult with long brown hair, different-colored eyes, and glasses. Your voice is different, and you call yourself *Lucy*. Of *course* I didn't recognize you."

His excuse is pathetic, just like him.

I lean forward. "You are *horrible* to Mom, Thomas."

"I know I am."

"You don't deserve her. I didn't even know you were married before her. I can't believe you let your *drunk, crazy* ex-wife into her home. And you don't even take care of her." I shake my head. "You want to know what I think? I think you want Emilia to *die*. I think you *wish* she had. Instead, you drove Meredith to kill herself. Ironic, isn't it?"

Thomas's face goes pale. Meredith was his weakness.

I twist the knife deeper.

"Because of your deplorable, selfish ways, you have lost the only two women who ever loved you. You drive Mom to a stroke, and Meredith would rather rot in hell then carry on with you; how does that make you feel? You are a disgusting, *horrible* person, Thomas."

Thomas surges out of his chair, lunging toward the sink.

I watch as he barely makes it before he vomits.

And for the first time in twenty years, I don't feel like the one who should be ashamed.

FORTY-SEVEN
THOMAS

Now

After retching in the sink, I turn to see James has left the kitchen to return to Emilia.

I vomit once more before finally retreating to my shop where I lie on the couch and stare at the ceiling in a weird, hypnotic daze.

My stepson. The ghost I buried years ago, now flesh and blood, upstairs next to the wife I discarded long ago. The ghost is back, a category five hurricane blowing into the life I built without him.

I think about my reputation. My career. My legacy. Everything I've spent the last twenty years building—it all hangs in the balance. I can already picture the headlines, the tabloid vultures circling, tearing apart my name, my carefully constructed life. The charities I represent, the endorsements, the adoring public who believes in the man I've shown them— what will they think when they learn the truth?

The weight of it crushes me. And for the first time in years, I feel something I thought I'd conquered: fear.

. . .

It's now seven in the morning. Wearing the same clothes I wore yesterday, I click on the small television in the corner of the kitchen and begin making coffee.

A *Breaking News* banner runs across the bottom on the screen and my stomach drops. Has word of my presumed-to-be dead stepson's return already gotten out?

Heart hammering, I grab the remote and turn it up.

"...update on the local house fire on County Road 615. Authorities have confirmed that human remains were found in the home. Samples have been sent for DNA testing. The body is presumed to belong to the missing long-time tenant of the home, Marcus Alvarez. As you know, last week, Alvarez didn't show up for work at the water treatment facility, the day following the fire. There were no other bodies found in the home. This is a rapidly unfolding story. Stay tuned. We'll bring you more information as soon as we..."

Relief flows through me. I exhale. No one knows—yet.

I'm pouring coffee when James steps into the kitchen. Despite knowing that I know he is my stepson, he is still Lucy, complete with different-colored contacts, glasses, and her voice.

With nothing more than a glance in my direction, James crosses the kitchen and makes himself a cup of coffee.

James drinks coffee now.

I watch in awe, unbelieving that he's here in my kitchen, making coffee. It's as if every bad decision, every regret I've ever had is standing right here next to me.

He sips, turns to me.

"So," he begins an obviously prepared speech, "I'm in a bit of a conundrum here. I can call the local news and tell them that I'm not dead, that I'm back, and that I have a story that will blow their socks off—or you and I can work something out."

"Like what?" I growl.

James smirks. "Figured you'd choose option number two. I'd sure hate to steal the spotlight from you." He winks, then, "So I'd like to fully take over Emilia's care, including her medication, from now forward."

The shock of his return hasn't allowed my thoughts to broach the question of "what now?" My head spins. So, this means James wants to stay? Of course he does. This house is a mansion compared to his Tahoe.

"Okay," I say. "I agree."

"Good." James leans against the counter, his expression passive but his gaze sharp. He doesn't appear to feel nearly as awkward or desperate as I do. He's either hiding it, or despises me so much that I am unworthy of triggering such emotion. It reminds me of Emilia's disposition toward the end. The woman didn't blink an eye at any of my shortcomings. She'd simply given up on me, on her life, on everything.

My stomach sours. I slide my coffee onto the counter.

"Also, I'd like a pay increase," he says.

My brows shoot up. "So you want to be paid to take care of your mother?"

"You paid me before you realized it was me. What difference does it make now?"

Okay. So it's going to be like this, then.

My hackles begin to raise. "Fine, James. How much would you like?"

He throws out a number, which I instantly agree to. I have a lot of money, after all, in case he needs a reminder of whose home he's in.

A long moment stretches between us and it becomes glaringly apparent that there is no father/stepson dynamic here. Instead, we are two grown men wading through a power shift. James clearly wants the upper hand, and plans to get it by using my ego against me. But I refuse to allow my stepson, who *willingly* left us, to steal the home I built without him.

"Anything else, James?"

"I'd like to know what really happened to Mom. Why she's so sick."

"She's not sick. She had a stroke. You—or Lucy, I should say—knows that."

"I don't believe you. The medications she's on aren't congruent with a stroke. She's sedated out of her mind."

"Are you a doctor now?"

James deadpans.

"Fine, James. You want the truth?"

"Yes."

"Are you sure you can handle it?"

"Yes."

I cross my arms over my chest. "Emilia tried to kill herself. She drowned herself in the bathtub before I came in and saved her. She'd been underwater without oxygen for long enough that she sustained permanent brain damage. This is the real reason she's unable to speak or move fluidly."

James is making a valiant effort to remain controlled, but I catch the flash of emotion in his face. The deep swallow of his throat. The set of his jaw. The pain in his eyes. I don't need to tell him that Emilia's decision to no longer be here was mostly because of the sustained torment she endured after he left us. Apparently, I'm not the only one with guilt. Good.

James forces back the emotions and clears his throat. I'm taken aback by how much the gesture reminds me of Emilia.

"I want to see the medical records," he demands.

"I have them on my computer. I'll print them out for you."

"Good. Why did you tell everyone she had a stroke?"

"To spare her the shame. Your mother made an unsuccessful attempt at suicide. I can't imagine she would want that information fed to gossips."

"You mean *you* wouldn't want that information to get out."

"Fine. Yes, you got me. It would make us all look bad."

"If it was a stroke, why is she so drugged?"

"Because she's trapped in her own body, James. We don't know how much she can understand or hear. We decided a long time ago that comfort was the best course of treatment for Emilia."

"Who's we?"

Me and Meredith—and her dealer, who was an expert at cloning prescription labels. But of course, I don't say that.

"Me and her doctor. I'm done with this conversation. Is there anything else?"

"Yes, there is something else. I want you to offer Consuelo a position as a live-in housekeeper."

This catches me off guard. "A *live-in?*"

He nods.

"Why?"

"She needs the money. And you obviously don't care to keep up the place on your own. I'll take care of Mom, Consuelo will take care of the house, and you're free to spend your days however you want."

"I spoke with her yesterday. She said she's going through some personal matters and needs more time off. I don't think she's ever coming back."

"An hourly raise will convince her."

"Fine," I say through clenched teeth. "She can stay in the guest room downstairs."

"In the bedroom your ex-wife died in? No."

I concede, mainly to end this maddening conversation. "Consuelo can stay in the guest room upstairs."

"Great. I'll call her now."

"Wait. What are you going to tell her—about you?"

"You mean am I going to tell her that my name is James, and I'm Emilia's long-lost son?"

Smartass.

"No. I'm not going to tell her."

"Why?"

"Because, Thomas," he jerks back his shoulders, reminding me of when he was a defiant teenager, "I like Lucy. Lucy is brave. She is finally facing her past."

FORTY-EIGHT

EMILIA

Now

Here's the thing about pills. They only work if you take them. Thomas's brazen disregard for my well-being had an unexpected silver lining. Many times, Thomas would forget to administer my medication. For days, sometimes. He'd get lost in his work, locked away in his shop, and forget about the less important things in his life—like me. During those times I'd wake from my drugged stupor to a haze of reality. To blurred lines of color that eventually morphed into objects. A door here, a window there, a lamp, my foot, my hand. A jarring juxtaposition of both confusion and awareness.

Today is no different. I awaken in the usual foggy, confused state.

Thomas forgot my pills again, I think. *Good.* Another opportunity to plan a way out of this hellish cage.

The scene around me begins to take shape—as it always does.

I'm sitting in the armchair, facing the mountains I wish to escape to. In front of me is James, his memory hovering over me like a sentinel. The image of him looks so real that it's jarring and I'm instantly thrust into flashbacks. When this happens—when I have flashbacks of my son—I'm flooded with a plethora of emotion. Not all are pleasant. Some days, there are happy memories of when James was a baby. The firsts, the milestones. Other days, the memories are of when he was a teenager. When he'd shut himself in his room and off from the world. That's when we grew apart.

Except today, James isn't a memory. He is standing in front of me, in full human form. But now, he has long brown hair, different-colored eyes, and glasses. But it's him. I'm sure of it. He's here, in this room, as present as my own beating heart.

My pulse begins to quicken, creating a dizzying rush through the drugged haze.

James is here.

James is here!

My fingernail scrapes the armrest faster, faster. My body wants to talk, to scream. To launch myself out of the chair and wrap my arms around my son. But I can't move.

A weeks-ago memory of Thomas introducing James to me as Lucy seeps in. Why? Why did he say his name was Lucy? It's not Lucy, it's my son. Yes, he looks different, but this is my son.

James stares down at me, his expression riddled with not only anxiety, but deep sadness.

I squeeze shut my eyes as another memory hits me, a much more recent one. This one is of me, after realizing Lucy was James, lunging for him as he walked into the room, so that he wouldn't leave again. So that I could tell him everything... And then I remember screaming. So much screaming. Then the sting of the needle...

"Mom." My son's voice cracks.

Mom.

Warmth spreads over my chest. *Mom.* That's who I used to be. *Mom.*

I look around. We're alone in the bedroom.

My son takes my hand and drops to his knees in front of me. He used to do this when I would be in one of my moods. When I'd retreat to the armchair, in the old house, to stare out the window and wonder when I'd let down my husband so much that he resorted to seeking affection from other women. James would look up at me, big eyes worried and wanting.

"Come outside with me, Mom. Let's play before Dad comes home."

He had the cutest lisp back then.

I'd force a smile, lean down and kiss his knuckles. *"Okay, but this time I'll be Rapunzel, and you'll be the wicked stepmom."*

He'd giggle and off we'd go. Escaping reality until it came barreling down the driveway. Then, we'd slip into our appropriate roles. Me, the loving wife; James, the doting stepson. But we both knew I was nothing more than a doormat, and James was nothing more than a disappointment.

James squeezes my hand, regaining my attention. "Mom, I am so sorry." His chin begins to quiver. "I'm *so sorry*, Mom, for what I put you through. I had no idea you tried to end your life." He takes a shuddered breath. "Yes, it's me, your son. James. I know you know. I know you weren't attacking me when you lunged at me from behind the door the other day," he whispers, his gaze flicking to the doorway behind us.

So my memory is accurate. It really happened. I did lunge at him. And also, Thomas must have told him about what really happened in that bathroom so long ago.

Tears pool in my eyes. I try to speak. I can't. Dammit, I want to speak!

"I know you were grabbing for me instead—because I know you recognize me. I can see it in your eyes now." His eyes fill with tears. "God, I am so, so sorry."

Unable to contain his emotion, James drops his forehead to our clasped hands and begins sobbing.

"I'm so sorry, Mom. I didn't know. I swear, I didn't know how bad you'd gotten. I promise, I didn't. You have to believe me. But I'm here now. What can I do, Mom? How can I help you?"

He can help me! My savior is here!

I tug out of his hold. My hand trembles as it lifts from the arm rest. Using all the energy I have, I propel myself forward, sweeping my arm across the rolling table that sits next to us. The prescription pill bottles tumble to the floor.

James startles and looks at me. Blinks.

"Oh," he says finally. "No more medicine. That's what you want. Okay, then... let's begin weaning then, shall we?"

My eyes close as a rush of relief expels from my lungs. I drop my head against the headrest and begin to weep.

FORTY-NINE
EMILIA

Now

"Mom, Mom!"

I'm faintly aware of being shaken. Of urgent whispers above my head. I squeeze my eyes, cursing the repeated movement on my shoulder. The noise. The brutal pain in my head.

I realize I'm wet. My nightgown is soaked. The bed underneath me is damp, too. I wonder if I wet the bed, but as quickly as the horrifying thought arises, it gets forgotten under the severe nausea consuming my body.

"Mom, Mom..."

Stop! Shut up! Shut up! I will my brain to tell my arm to lift and cover my ears, but the communication gets lost in transit. I am so sick I can't move.

"Mom, you're screaming!" The voice hisses above me. *"You're having another nightmare; we don't want to wake up Thomas..."*

Thomas.

James. The voice above me is James. My son. Lucy.

We don't want to wake up Thomas...

No, we definitely don't want that to happen. The thought of it gives me a jolt of adrenaline.

James gently rolls me onto my back. The movement is a slow but violent wave crashing through my body. I unfold out of the fetal position. Beads of sweat roll down the sides of my legs, slithering out of the creases of my knees.

A cold, wet washcloth is laid on my forehead.

I moan in appreciation.

"Good job, Mom. You can take more ibuprofen now. I think this is the worst of it." James gently strokes my hair. Like I did to him when he was little.

Once the room stops spinning, I squint into the darkness. We don't risk turning on lights during my nighttime episodes, because we don't want to raise suspicion.

Once I confirm the door is shut—and Thomas isn't anywhere to be seen—I drag in a long, deep inhale.

The withdrawals I'm having from my medication is something I wouldn't wish on my worst enemy. Dizziness that turns into vertigo. Migraine. Nausea. Day and night vomiting. In hindsight, yes, we should have weaned much slower. But there was no other option. Mainly because I don't know how long James will be here and I need him here to get me off my medication. Therefore, weaning in an appropriate timeframe was not an option. Also, I'm desperate to be rid of the poison that has kept me locked in this cage, and if I have to vomit my way through the process, so be it. With every pain or wave of nausea, I remind myself that I am one step closer to being clean. To being able to walk myself out of this godforsaken glass house.

The withdrawals have been difficult to hide from Thomas. I spend most of my time on the cold tiles of the bathroom floor with my knees wrapped around the toilet. We've begun keeping the bedroom door shut—and locked.

It's been hard on James, too. He's become worried enough

about me that he's threatened to halt the weaning for another week, to ease my discomfort.

I refuse.

James is different today. More anxious than usual. We're in the bathroom, our usual spot. Instead of reading to me as he usually does to distract me, he is curled up next to me, quietly sketching.

It reminds me of the months before he ran away. James would lock himself in his room to sketch for hours.

Scattered on the floor between us are a dozen paintings and a book filled with drawings. Many replicas of Van Gogh's famous paintings.

Finally, he drops the pad.

A long, heavy moment fills the room. I want to pull myself off the floor, into a seated position, but I can't even raise my cheek from the cold tiles.

Finally, he speaks. "Mom, how well do you know Consuelo?"

I picture the beautiful housekeeper. The one my husband hired without consulting me so long ago. I swallow to speak, but my throat burns from dry heaving. Also, finding my voice again has been more difficult than I anticipated.

He continues, "You remember how I told you Meredith overdosed downstairs? And that the cops think it's a suicide?"

I nod, and even that small movement hurts.

"Well... I keep wondering if it really *was* suicide. Meredith was too spirited, too obsessed with Thomas. I didn't get the vibe that she was at the end of her rope—not at all. So, if she didn't mean to end her life, that means someone else did it for her. And there are only two people in this house who could have done it. Thomas or Consuelo." He pauses, chewing on his lip. "I truly do not think Thomas did it. I think he liked her being here. She did whatever he wanted her to do, whenever he wanted it— if you know what I mean."

I roll my eyes and fight another dry heave.

"So that leaves Consuelo. I know that Meredith had threatened to turn her in to immigration. They obviously hated each other. Also, Consuelo told me she grew up in a rough neighborhood and that violence has always been a part of her life, and..." He looks at me. "Did you know her boyfriend gets rough with her?"

I shake my head, barely.

"He does, and maybe she just snapped." He heaves out a heavy sigh. "Lastly, Consuelo hasn't been back here since it happened, which is really strange." He shrugs, though his expression is pulled in deep thought. "I don't know. It's just weird. I have a strange feeling that there is more to Consuelo than meets the eye. That she knows something, or has done something that is keeping her away." His eyes narrow. "Like poison Meredith."

FIFTY
EMILIA

Now

Four days later, finally, the withdrawals subside, and the haze lifts. Clarity has swept in, piece by piece, and for the first time in years, I can speak—truly speak out loud. Words form in my mind, crisp and coherent, where before there had only been a murky blur. I've been able to mutter to James, but not much more than a few words.

It's a pitch-black, cold night. The chill seeps into my bones, mingling with the lingering exhaustion from the war my body fought the last few days. In bed, I lean against the pillows, every muscle aching. The evening news plays low on the television in the corner. We keep it on so that Thomas won't hear us speak, but we needn't worry. Thomas hasn't visited the second floor a single time since he discovered Lucy is his son. According to James, they rarely speak or see each other.

I can only imagine how this revelation has affected Thomas. It must have shattered the carefully constructed narrative he built when he declared James dead so long ago. But despite everything, I feel nothing for him—no sympathy, no sorrow. He made his choices. He chose who to love and who to cast away.

And here we are, the two castaways, finding each other once again.

James sits beside me on the bed, his presence a steady anchor in this fragile moment. His patience has been unyielding, carrying me through the long stretches of silence when words felt impossible. He's been waiting for me to come to this place, not just physically but mentally, to become whole enough to engage with the world again.

I turn to my son, take in his profile as he watches the news. The past between us, raw and painful, still lingers, but for the first time, it doesn't feel insurmountable. There is something else now—hope.

He and I. A team.

I draw in a deep breath. The kind of breath you take when you're about to step into the unknown, knowing there's no turning back.

"James... I want to thank you," I whisper. "Thank you for helping me through this, for being here, for your patience until I felt strong enough to talk." I reach out, grab his hand. "James, it's time we share all the secrets between us. What do you say?"

He smiles. "Sharing secrets appears to be the theme in this house."

"Okay I'll go first." I swallow deeply. "You know that your father has been negligent with my medications for years, but it's not just that. He's been sedating me using drugs Meredith provided him."

"I knew it!" James hisses.

"Shh." I press my finger to my lips. "How did you know?"

"I didn't know that Meredith was providing them, but I knew you were under *way* too much sedation. I asked Thomas to see your medical records, but he never showed me, and I didn't follow up because I knew he could've forged them himself and I wouldn't know the difference. Wait." He frowns. "How do you know about it?"

The memory comes back hot, like a cattle prod in my side. "They spoke about it standing over my bed when they thought I was blacked out."

James shakes his head.

"I heard so much more than they thought I did." I take a deep breath. "Anyway, during the days that Thomas would forget to sedate me, one thing became apparent. I needed help. I needed someone to get me far away from my abusive husband. I attempted to breach the realm of nonverbal communication with Consuelo. But each time I attempted to 'speak' to her, she misconstrued the effort as pain and would call Thomas to come check on me. Minutes later, I'd be injected once again, and slip back into the dreamless world in which I lived.

"For years this went on. Until one day, memories began to trickle into my wakeful states. I believe my brain was beginning to heal and it was like a drip of flashbacks, each one weaving the story that led me to this godawful place..." My voice trails off, the memories becoming too vivid. Too sickening.

"Tell me, Mom." James grabs my hand, his eyes glistening. "Tell me everything."

And I do. I tell him about how Thomas threatened to frame me for Eugene's murder multiple times, trapping me in this abusive, loveless marriage.

"This is when I decided to end my life." My heart begins to hammer, but I press on. "As luck would have it—or wouldn't— Thomas got there just in time to save me. If you consider this," I gesture to the bed, "saved."

"Mom, I am so, so sorry." James begins to weep. "It's all my fault."

"No it's not. James, look at me." I sit up, pull my legs into criss-cross under the covers and face him fully. "You left to get away from Thomas. I tried to end my life to get away from him.

We both ran away, just in different ways. I completely, one hundred percent understand why you did what you did. I only wish I had been smart enough to leave with you."

He wipes his eyes with the back of his hand. "Thank you for understanding."

"I do, son, more than you know. So that's my truth. Now it's time for yours. Why didn't you ever come back, James? Why didn't you try to contact me?"

His shoulders hunch forward, eyes fixed on our clasped hand. The weight and pain of years apart hangs heavy in the air between us.

"I was scared," he admits, his voice breaking. "I was scared Thomas would hurt you, like he hurt Eugene. Every time I thought about contacting you, I'd stop myself, telling myself I was protecting you by not reaching out. I didn't know what else to do." His words come faster now, like a dam breaking. "I was a kid. I really thought I was protecting you. And also, as the months dragged on, I became ashamed. Ashamed for not being able to stand up to him, for running away, for leaving you. The longer I was gone, the harder it was to reach out. Eventually, I thought I didn't deserve to come back."

Tears sting my eyes, but I don't let them fall. "James, you didn't have to protect me. I'm your mother. It was my job to protect you, and I failed miserably."

"Well, so did I, Mom. I hurt you, and myself, too." His voice wavers, and he wipes at his face roughly, like he's angry at himself for crying.

I pull James into my arms, and for the first time in years, my son clings to me tightly, like he's afraid I might let go.

"I'm sorry, Mom," he whispers again, his voice muffled against my shoulder.

"I'm sorry, too," I whisper back, stroking his hair like I used to when he was little. "You're home now. That's all that matters. You're home, and we're going to be okay."

We sit there in silence for a long time, the years of pain and separation slowly dissolving in the warmth of our embrace.

What feels like a lifetime, yet not nearly long enough later, James pulls away.

He looks at me, intently, the tears replaced by a sharp, resolute look in his eyes.

"Mom," he says, "We have to get you out of here."

I nod. "We *both* have to get out of here."

FIFTY-ONE
EMILIA

Now

I've just closed my eyes for a nap when the door bursts open.

I jolt upright, my heart slamming against my ribs as James rushes in, breathless. His eyes are wide.

"Mom." His voice is hushed but urgent. He closes the door behind him, the soft *click* echoing through the stillness.

I push myself up on my elbows. "What's wrong?"

"I went downstairs to make a snack," he says, his voice barely above a whisper. He glances over his shoulder as if someone might be standing in the shadows, before crossing the room.

"And?" I urge, my voice steady despite the unease crawling up my spine.

"There was a gun on the kitchen table," he breathes. "Just lying there. In the center."

I feel the blood drain from my face. The pistol Thomas used to blackmail me for years. Now, a warning.

"It freaked me out," James continues, "and when I looked down the hallway... he was there. Thomas. He was just *standing* there, Mom. Arms crossed, in the shadows. Watching me with this intense look on his face."

I grip the blanket, my fingers digging into the fabric.

"He wanted me to see it," James continues. "I know he did."

"I'm afraid you're right. He wants you to remember," I say, my gaze shifting to the doorway.

"Remember what?"

I meet his gaze, the weight of the years pressing down on me. "That this is *his* house," I whisper. "And he is the master of it."

As James stares at me, I wonder if tonight really is just a warning—

Or the beginning of something much, much worse.

FIFTY-TWO

EMILIA

Now

"Mom, you're doing it!" James squeaks with excitement. "This is your tenth lap around the room! You don't even need me!"

I smile—beam, more like—my head hanging low as I watch my socked feet glide across the hardwood floor. Each step feels monumental, a triumph against the weight of my own broken body. Yes, I am doing it. I have walked ten laps around the bedroom at a strong, quick pace—*all on my own.*

I bask in James's delight. It's been too long since I felt in control of my own movements, my own life. There's still a long road ahead, but today marks a significant victory. My muscles are getting stronger, and the withdrawals are completely gone— and Thomas still has no idea what we've been doing up here. What an oblivious, self-absorbed bastard he is.

James has been my lifeline through all of this. He's been more than a son—he's been my coach, my cheerleader, my quiet strength. As I struggled to move, he educated himself, watching endless videos on in-home physical therapy, learning techniques to help me regain control. We've spent four grueling hours each day working through exercises. Each session leaves me drained, but it's working. Soon, we'll attempt the stairs.

Everything is falling into place.

"Come on, let's get you back to the chair," James says gently, guiding me back to the recliner.

I drop into the armchair with a long, relieved exhale.

"That was so good, Mom." James kneels in front of me, his eyes shining with pride. He strokes my forearm gently. "Tomorrow, we'll figure out a way to do the stairs. Oh! And I spoke with the physical therapy place in town. Don't worry, I didn't use your name or mine. I just gave them a brief overview of your condition—specifically your muscle atrophy. They said they could take a new client without any issues. They estimate six to eight months of treatment to rebuild your strength. But we'll figure all that out..."

My lips part in shock. Six to eight months!

His words fade as I close my eyes, the joy instantly replaced by devastation. Six to eight months until I'm a fully capable adult again. The consequences of Thomas's malevolent neglect will last long after I'm free of him. Hate—vile, putrid, white-hot hatred—slowly simmers in my stomach, but I push it away and remind myself that, soon enough, he will no longer control me.

I remind myself of my inner grit. The inner strength that no one—not even Thomas—can take away. Six to eight months will be okay. It has to be. I've lived in this cage for years. I can handle six to eight more months.

James stands. "You need to rest now."

Our gaze shifts to the window that overlooks the driveway.

"Have you heard from Consuelo?" I ask.

He shakes his head, eyes darkening. "No. I've called her every day since she left. She's stopped taking my calls. I'm telling you, I really think she had something to do with Meredith's death. Why else would she be staying away?" He shakes his head, as if shaking away the bad energy. "Rest, Mom. I'll make you some tea. Be right back."

"James," I call his name as he crosses the room. "Don't forget—be careful. Thomas can't find out what we're doing. If he suspects anything, we're in real danger."

"I know, Mom. I'll be careful. I promise."

FIFTY-THREE
EMILIA

Now

The late-afternoon light creeps through the blinds, casting slanted light across the floor. I sit on the edge of the bed, watching James as he double-checks the forecast on the laptop. His brow furrows in concentration, his fingers swiping through charts and radar maps. We can't afford any surprises.

"It looks like the storm is moving in faster than we'd anticipated," he says, keeping his voice low. "It will be here tomorrow afternoon."

Tomorrow.

We stare at each other, the reality settling between us like a lead weight.

Tomorrow.

James swallows, returns his attention to the screen. "Today is going to be warm and a little windy, but nothing that would stop us from practicing."

"Good," I reply, flexing my fingers. They're sore, but it's a good kind of sore—the kind that means I'm getting stronger. We don't have much time left. The weather is coming. The window is closing, and we can't wait for another opportunity.

This is it.

James stands, stretching his lanky frame. He's grown taller than I'd guessed he would have, and despite being dressed as Lucy, there's still a boyishness about him that catches me off guard sometimes. I hate that he's part of this, that he has to bear the weight of something so dark and dangerous. But there's no other way. We're in this together.

"Ready for another workout?" he asks, lowering his voice even more.

I nod, slipping into a pair of sneakers I haven't worn in years. My muscles ache from yesterday's drills, but pain doesn't matter. Pain is temporary. Failure isn't an option.

James walks to the door and peeks out into the hallway, listening for any sound from below.

"Has he even come out of his shop?"

James rolls his eyes. "No. I think he sleeps in there. Okay. We're all clear," he whispers, gesturing for me to follow.

Carefully, I rise from the bed, every movement deliberate. James takes the lead, his footsteps light as he approaches the staircase. We've done this before—sneaking up and down the stairs when Thomas runs into town for groceries—but it's never felt as urgent as it does now.

"I'll keep watch at the bottom," James says, jogging down the staircase. Once in place, he leans slightly over the banister, peering at the hallway that leads to Thomas's shop.

He gives me a thumbs up.

Taking a deep breath, I place my hand on the railing. The wood feels cool under my palm. I lift my foot and set it down on the first step, making sure not to make a sound. Slowly, carefully, I shift my weight forward. The stair creaks softly, and I freeze, my heart pounding in my chest. James glances back at me, giving a slight nod to continue.

Step by step, I climb down, each movement precise and controlled. My legs burn from the strain, but I push through it. I have to. There's no room for weakness now.

Halfway down, I hear a faint sound—the distant creak of a floorboard. My breath catches in my throat, and I look at James. He holds up a hand, signaling me to wait. His eyes narrow as he listens intently. After a moment, he relaxes and waves me on.

When I reach the bottom, I grip the railing tightly, my legs trembling from the effort.

"You okay?" James whispers.

I nod. "Let's keep going."

He guides me to the hallway leading to the back door. This stretch is crucial. If Thomas hears us or catches us here, everything we've worked for will fall apart.

"Ready?" James asks, his voice steady despite the tension in the air.

"Ready," I whisper back.

We move in unison, our steps perfectly synchronized. The hallway feels longer than it ever has before, every shadow seeming to stretch and reach toward us. My breath comes in shallow bursts, but I keep going.

When we finally reach the back door, I lean against the wall, letting out a long, shaky exhale. James smiles proudly.

"You did great, Mom," he says softly. "Tomorrow, we'll run the route again first thing in the morning. One last time."

One last time.

FIFTY-FOUR

EMILIA

Now

The morning is gray and bleak with the impending storm. Dim light filters through the thin curtains, casting a pale glow across the room. It's quiet, almost unnervingly so, as if the world itself is holding its breath.

Slowly, awakening, I stare at the ceiling, my mind already racing ahead to what the day holds.

Today is the day.

James is sitting in the chair by the window. His arms rest on his knees, and his hands are clasped together tightly. He's been awake for a while. His shoulders are tense but he's trying to stay calm, trying to be strong—for both of us.

For a moment, I stare out the window, reflecting on my time here in this godforsaken house of glass. The windows stretch from the floor to the ceiling, spotless and unyielding, framing the outside world like a painting I could never touch. For years I stared out these windows at the sea of green, taunting me with a freedom I could never have. It was torture. The worst part was the silence. Unlike the view outside, there was no hum of life inside—no birdsong, no rustling leaves, no scent of fresh air. This house, with all its opulence and brilliance, was a tomb.

Today all that changes.

"Morning," I say softly, my voice breaking the silence.

James glances over, offering a small, tight-lipped smile. "Morning."

For a moment, neither of us speak.

"We can do this," I say, sitting up and swinging my legs over the side of the bed. James rises and joins me at the side of the bed. "We've planned for this. We've prepared. We've gone over every detail a hundred times."

James nods, his eyes locked on mine. "We can't mess it up, Mom. If we do—"

"We won't," I reply firmly. I reach out, taking his hand in mine. His grip is strong, steady. "We're in this together, James. No matter what happens, we stick to the plan. No hesitation, no second-guessing. Just like we practiced."

"Right." He exhales, running a hand through his hair. "No backing out. No mistakes."

"No mistakes," I echo.

Thoughtfully, he runs his thumb over the back of my hand. "You know what kept me going through all of this? You. Us. For you and I to be able to live a life without fear."

I squeeze his hand, a burst of adrenaline—strength— charging through me. "And we're going to have that, James. After today, everything changes. We're going to be okay."

"Yes, we are," he agrees. "Together."

Together.

We stand, side by side, ready to face whatever comes. There's no turning back now. Today is the day—the day we take our lives into our own hands.

"Are you ready to send the text?"

James's eyes narrow.

He nods.

FIFTY-FIVE
JAMES

Now

I sit on the bench overlooking the ravine, the wind carrying a chill that digs into my skin. The sky churns with heavy, dark clouds, flickering with distant lightning. The storm is about to break loose.

Tiny raindrops gather in the carved letters on the bench: *Thomas and Emilia Forever.*

Liar.

A sharp crack pierces the silence behind me, the unmistakable snap of a twig. I close my eyes and inhale deeply, steadying the tremor in my hands.

"Hey." My stepfather's voice drifts through the air. "I just got your text."

I glance over my shoulder. Thomas steps out of the tree line, the navy-blue hood of his raincoat pulled low over his face. Mist coils through the forest like a living thing, curling around his legs as he approaches.

A crow shrieks above us, its black wings slicing through the fog before diving into the ravine.

Thomas holds up a raincoat. "Thought you might need this."

When I don't take it, he drapes it over the backrest of the bench. He doesn't sit. Instead, he stands beside the bench, hands stuffed into his jeans pockets.

We stare across the ravine.

Finally, he speaks. "So, what's this about?"

"We need to discuss something."

"Fine." His impatience flares; I can feel it radiating off him. "Let's start here: what are your intentions here, James?"

"To take care of Mom," I say, my voice measured. "You know that."

"Bullshit. How much do you want?"

"Are you asking me to leave?"

"Yes." His response is instant, cold. "You abandoned this family, James. You ran off and left your mother to deal with the aftermath. Simply because you felt slighted by me. You put your wounded pride over your mother's mental and physical well-being for all these years. There is not a single part of me that believes you're here because you want to take care of her."

"You're a manipulative son of a bitch, you know that?"

He ignores the jab. "Tell me your price, and then get out."

"What's the price tag for calling your son a faggot and driving your wife to kill herself?"

The tension—the *hatred*—between us is palpable.

"I'm not having this conversation. Name your number."

"I'm not leaving Mom, Thomas."

"Yes. You are." He turns fully toward me. Underneath the shadow of his hood, his eyes glint like a predator circling its prey. "You want money? Fine. You want revenge for all the ways I've failed you? Consider this your win. But you'll take the money and go, and never return. And you won't say a word to anyone about me or this family."

The storm rumbles overhead.

"I'm not leaving," I say again, as leaves rustle behind us.

My adrenaline surges.

I let out a slow breath to steady my voice. "The thing is, *Dad*, I'm not the only one who wants revenge."

On cue, Emilia bursts from the shadows of the tree line, her movements frantic and raw. She's soaked, her baggy sweatpants clinging to her bony legs, her face twisted in unbridled rage.

Thomas barely has time to process what's happening.

"Emilia?" he breathes, his voice breaking for the first time.

A guttural scream rips through the air as Emilia throws her full weight into his chest, shoving him with every bit of force she has in her.

Thomas stumbles backward, losing his footing.

Emilia collapses to the ground, exhausted, but she's done her part.

It's my turn.

Already in position, I grip the bench for leverage as I stretch out my leg, meeting Thomas's staggering steps.

He trips over my foot.

His eyes, wide with shock, lock onto mine.

A scream rips from his throat as his body tumbles over the edge.

FIFTY-SIX
EMILIA

Now

I press my palm against the cool, rain-streaked window, releasing the heat from my skin. My reflection stares back at me, pale and gaunt, eyes ringed with shadows.

Beyond the glass, the storm rages. The wind howls, bending trees, and spinning leaves into the air. I picture my husband's body at the bottom of the ravine being battered by the rain.

He's gone.

I let the thought settle, testing it again. Saying it in my head doesn't make it less surreal.

He's. Gone.

For years, I imagined this moment—what it would feel like, how I might react. I told myself I'd be free, finally unshackled. And I am—but there's a hollowness in my chest, one I didn't expect. It's not grief because grief implies love or loss, and Thomas doesn't deserve either.

It's guilt.

Yes, I hated my husband. He was cruel, cold, manipulative. He chipped away at me until I was nothing but fragments. And yet, as much as I despised him, there was a time when I loved him, or at least believed I did.

The rain is falling harder now, hammering against the glass like it's trying to alert me that there's a dead man outside.

I close my eyes, reminding myself of the pain he caused my son. Myself. The actual prison he kept me in, the emotional one he'd kept James in.

Thomas is not worthy of my guilt.

I owe him nothing. Not my tears, not my sadness, not my regret.

He's gone, and I can release it all now.

I can breathe again.

Finally.

FIFTY-SEVEN
JAMES

Now

When I return from the bathroom, freshly changed into dry clothes, Emilia is in her armchair. She's abandoned the sweatshirt and pants she wore at the ravine for a soft house dress. Her damp hair clings to her temples in limp, blonde strands. She's clutching a photograph, one I instantly recognize. It's the picture of her and her mother, barefoot and laughing, stomping grapes in a vineyard in Italy.

Emilia's gaze is fixed on the window, staring in the direction of the ravine, where Thomas fell—or rather, where we made him fall. Her expression is thoughtful, reflective.

I wasn't sure what to expect from my mother after we finished the job. We'd planned it down to the last detail, but planning an act and living with it are entirely different beasts.

I move behind her chair and gently stroke her hair. My eyes fall to the photograph in her hands.

"You miss your mom," I say quietly.

"Every day," she whispers.

"And Italy. You miss Italy, too."

"Every day."

I step around the chair and kneel at her feet. "Well, now you can go back, Mom. He doesn't control you anymore. You can do anything—be anyone. Go anywhere."

A ghost of a smile across her lips, fragile but real. "I've been thinking the same thing." She nods to her skeletal leg. "As soon as I get stronger."

"You will. And when you are, you should do it. Make it a fresh start."

"A life do-over." Her voice is soft, almost wistful. "And you, son? What will you do?"

"Come with you? Is that what you're asking?" I wink. "No. I've got my own adventures to chase."

She nods, her smile faint but bittersweet. "You're just like me, you know that?"

The sudden sound of movement downstairs jolts both of us from the moment, as I stand instantly. For a split second, I imagine it's Thomas resurrected, crawling back from the ravine to kill us all.

I rush to the window.

"It's Consuelo," I say, my pulse kicking.

"Consuelo?" Emilia's voice sharpens, matching my own unease. "How long has she been here?"

"I don't know. I didn't see when she pulled up. We've been up here for what—two hours? What if she saw us coming back from the cliff? What if she saw everything?"

Emilia's face tightens, but she doesn't waste time. We've come too far to have things messed up for us now. She pushes herself out of the chair, her movements slow but urgent, and crawls into bed. Consuelo expects her to be weak, bedridden, drugged into oblivion. It's time for her to play the part, one more time. And for myself too, because Consuelo doesn't know I'm James. She thinks I'm Lucy.

Adrenaline pumps as I tuck the blankets around Emilia's

frail frame, pulling them up to her neck. "Okay, let's run through this again. If Consuelo asks where Thomas is, I'll tell her he's locked in his shop, like always. She'll buy that. And remember, I'm still Lucy—she doesn't know I'm James, your son. She also doesn't know you're lucid. To her, you're still sedated, barely able to speak or move. Got it?"

Emilia nods, adjusting the pillow behind her.

"Good. And the plan hasn't changed. We'll call the police tomorrow to report Thomas missing. The rain will back up the story—that he must have slipped and fell. The storm will wash away our prints, and any trace of us on him."

Footsteps on the staircase.

Quickly, I lean close to Emilia, whispering, "We just have to stay cool, Mom. He's gone. This is our house now. You and me. I've got you."

She nods, her eyes locked on mine. For a moment, I see the faintest flicker of pride beneath the fear.

I straighten, and take a quick glance in the mirror, confirming I still look like Lucy.

"Come in."

Consuelo steps inside, her sharp, probing gaze immediately landing on Emilia. She looks harder than usual, her expression intense, like she's searching for something.

"Everything okay up here?" she asks, her voice clipped.

I force a casual smile. "Yeah. Why?"

"Just checking." Her eyes linger on Emilia, and I feel my stomach twist.

"Are you coming back to work?" I ask.

After an agonizing pause, "Yes. I sent Thomas a text this morning that I was coming back today. He didn't tell you?"

"No, he didn't. Are you going to stay here?"

"Not tonight. I'm staying with a friend. Okay... I'll check on you both again later." She looks at me, her eyes narrowing slightly. "Lucy, can we talk later?"

My throat tightens. "Of course."

Her gaze flickers back to Emilia before she leaves. The door clicks shut behind her, leaving the tension thick in the room.

We're safe for now, but apparently the storm isn't over.

Not yet.

FIFTY-EIGHT
JAMES

Now

After drawing Emilia a bath, I slip into the bedroom next door, still unnerved by Consuelo's sudden reappearance, and also riddled with anxiety that she might know what we did.

I remember checking the driveway before Emilia and I snuck to the ravine. Consuelo wasn't here. And yet... the way she looked at Emilia—sharp, searching, like she was trying to see into her. It doesn't sit right. She knows *something*.

If she knows what we did to Thomas, why hasn't she called the cops? Why not address it the moment she walked into the room? Why play this game instead? Tell me we need to "talk later?" The thought makes my stomach twist into a knot. Maybe she's toying with me, waiting for me to slip. Maybe she's biding her time.

Or maybe... maybe she doesn't know at all, and I'm unraveling over nothing.

Or is it that she's come to confess poisoning Meredith?

I sink onto the edge of the bed and drop my head into my

hands. I need to think clearly. The plan was perfect. Everything went according to our plan.

Right?

The question dangles in the air, unanswered. I close my eyes and run through it again, step by step, replaying every detail. The rain. The ravine. His body falling into the shadows below. Emilia's trembling hand gripping mine as we climbed back up. The rain will wash everything clean. It always does.

I exhale slowly, telling myself it's fine. Consuelo wasn't there. She didn't see. She can't know.

Everything went to plan.

Didn't it?

FIFTY-NINE
JAMES

Now

I sit propped against the headboard, an opened book in my lap. Emilia sleeps beside me, her face peaceful in the dim light of the room. My gaze is fixed on the bedroom door, waiting for Consuelo to summon me for the "talk" she requested earlier. But she hasn't come—and it's driving me crazy.

The ten o'clock news plays in the background. A flashing *Breaking News* banner runs across the top.

"*...an update on the remains found in the house fire on County Road 615...*"

That fire—I remember the story playing on the kitchen television the morning after Thomas discovered my compass and realized who I was.

I carefully lean over, pluck the remote from the comforter, and turn it up a notch.

"*DNA testing has confirmed that the remains found in the home belong to the missing man, Marcus Alvarez...*"

Marcus Alvarez. The name feels familiar, but I can't place it. My brow furrows as I try to recall where I've heard the name.

The story ends, replaced by a piece about local animal shelters, but the name loops in my head.

I *know* it. But how?

I switch off the television, lie back, and stare at the ceiling. My thoughts drift back to Consuelo. Why hasn't she come up to talk to me? Has she noticed Thomas isn't in his shop? What is she doing? What *does* she know? The questions churn, one feeding the next, as I dissect every conversation we've ever had together.

I bolt upright, gasping.

I remember how I know that name.

Marcus is—*was*—Consuelo's abusive boyfriend.

Her words echo in my mind. *"My boyfriend abused me, okay?... Marcus and I have been together, on and off, for a long time..."*

I grab the remote, turning the television back on, and rewinding the news. *"...remains found in the house fire on County Road 615..."*

County Road 615 isn't far from here, maybe fifteen or twenty minutes. I know that Consuelo lives twenty minutes away in a rental with her boyfriend—she told me so herself.

The pieces slide into place with brutal clarity. The fire happened the same weekend Consuelo said she was going to take some time off. A road trip, she'd said. And right before that, I saw her loading up two of Thomas's gas cans.

I set the remote onto the nightstand and scramble from the bed, grabbing the laptop. I pull up the original story from the local news website. The timeline definitely matches. The fire. Her weekend trip. The gas cans. *Oh my God.*

Consuelo killed her boyfriend.

This changes *everything*.

If Consuelo knows what happened to Thomas, I now have leverage. She, too, has blood on her hands. But how do I prove it?

And really, do I even need to? Am I spinning for no reason? After all, I'm only assuming Consuelo knows about Thomas. I don't know for certain, aside from a nagging gut feeling.

I pace the room, chewing my nails to the quick. How could she have seen what Emilia and I did?

Then it hits me.

"The security company is coming soon to fix some of the cameras. I need to transfer some files before they do."

The security cameras! Consuelo has access to them all. Despite telling me she doesn't look at the videos, I'm sure she did. Who wouldn't? She must have checked the footage when she arrived earlier today.

Shit.

I drop into the chair, my pulse thundering in my ears as the questions crash into me. Why hasn't she called the cops? Why mess with me instead?

And then another thought, one even more sinister, comes to mind.

If Consuelo is capable of killing her abusive boyfriend, then she is certainly capable of killing Meredith, too. After all, Meredith threatened to have her deported.

I *knew* it.

I stand, begin pacing. My gaze drifts to the dark bay windows. Quietly, I cross the room. The dark shapes of trees sway in the faint breeze, their shadows stretching across the lawn.

My breath fogs the glass as I stare at her car, mind racing.

I'm not sure how long I stand there, thinking, plotting, spinning, when movement catches my eye. Consuelo crosses the driveway with purpose, her bag slung over one shoulder, her keys clenched tightly in her hand. She pauses before opening the door, her head tilting upward. Our eyes meet through the darkness, and my heart stutters. Tension swirls between us, tangible even across the distance.

I lift a hand in questioning: *I thought you wanted to talk?*

Tomorrow, she mouths, then slips into the car and disappears into the night.

SIXTY
JAMES

Now – The Next Morning

"Nine one one what's your emergency?"

"I'd like to report a missing person."

"What is your first and last name?"

"Lucy Greer."

"Lucy, is the number you're calling from a good call-back number in case we get disconnected?"

"Yes."

"Okay. What's the name of the missing person?"

"Thomas Caine."

A brief pause. "Okay. What is your relationship with Mr. Caine?"

"I'm his employee."

"What do you do for him?"

"I'm a live-in caregiver for his wife."

"When was the last time you saw Mr. Caine?"

"Um, two days ago, I think. In the kitchen. I haven't seen him since."

"Have you confirmed that he's not in the home?"

"Yes. He usually works in his shop all day and all night. I assumed that's where he's been. But I became concerned this morning, so I went looking for him and he's not in his shop."

"You're in the home now?"

"Yes. I live here, like I said."

"Is his vehicle at the residence?"

"Yes. That's what I thought was strange. His car is here but I can't find him anywhere. Also, his phone is here, which I also thought was strange because if he had gone somewhere, why wouldn't he take his phone?"

"Okay, Miss Greer, we'll send an officer out shortly."

SIXTY-ONE

JAMES

Now

I pace the foyer, my heart racing like a runaway train. Outside, a dreary, gray mist has settled in the woods. More spring storms on the way. A car emerges from the trees, its headlights piercing the fog. Not a police car. It's Consuelo.

Shit. I can't deal with this right now.

She parks in her usual spot and steps out, a bag slung over her shoulder. My nerves are already frayed, and having a confrontation with Consuelo is the last thing I need right now.

This next phase of the plan must go perfectly. She cannot mess it up.

Last night, while Emilia slept and after Consuelo left, I went in search of the security hub because I needed to see for myself what Consuelo had seen on the cameras. I found it exactly where Consuelo said it was—adjacent to the media room, hidden behind a triple-locked door. After that fruitless endeavor, I returned to the laptop in Emilia's room, searching for a security app hidden somewhere on it. I know that these days many home security systems have their own apps where the owner can click in anytime. But I found nothing.

I gave up around four in the morning.

Consuelo steps inside, her boots clicking softly on the floor as her eyes lock on me—Lucy—standing by the window. A moment stretches between us, taut as a wire about to snap.

"What are you doing?" she asks, her gaze sharp.

"Waiting on the cops."

Her bag drops to the floor with a dull thud. "Why?"

Time to slip into the role, into the plan. "Because I haven't seen Thomas in two days."

The silence that follows is unbearable.

"What did you want to talk to me about last night?" I ask.

She pauses as if weighing how to proceed.

There is zero question in my mind anymore. The tension between us is too electric. Something big is happening. She knows.

Finally, she says, "I wanted to talk to you about the security footage."

My pulse is pounding so violently I think I might faint. "What about it?"

Consuelo crosses the room, closing the gap between us. "Do you remember when I told you the security company was coming and I needed to transfer some files?"

I nod, words caught in my throat.

"I lied to you when I said I didn't check the videos. Of course I did—I mean for the first time, I did. I haven't before, but after Emilia's crazy outburst when she attacked you, I just felt compelled to see what the hell was going on. I only went through a handful, but..." Her brows arch. "I saw *a lot* more than I should have. Thomas and Meredith were drugging Emilia. They were giving her sedatives on top of her prescribed meds."

I blink. Is that it? Is *that* what she knows? Relief flutters briefly in my chest, but her gaze tells me there's more. Because of course there is—there's *always* more.

Consuelo continues, "I was so shocked, so sickened, that I couldn't come back to work. That's why I took extended time off. I needed to figure out what, if anything, I was going to do. Eventually, I realized I had to address it. It's abuse." Her gaze narrows. "Did you know?"

"I sensed it."

She nods, then, "Where is she now?"

"Upstairs. Asleep." My answer is automatic, the lie slipping out with practiced ease. Consuelo can't know Emilia is awake, lucid, and more capable than anyone would believe.

Consuelo pauses again, and the anticipation becomes unbearable.

"Just say it, Consuelo," I blurt. "Whatever it is, just say it."

"Last night, I copied the files of Thomas and Meredith agreeing to drug Emilia onto a thumb drive so I would have evidence if I went to the cops. That's what was I going to talk to you about last night." Her eyes narrow. "But then, while going through the files, I saw something else."

There it is. The truth is finally out. She knows.

I swallow deeply, considering my options. Bottom line, I don't have leverage because I don't know for certain that Consuelo killed her abusive boyfriend—or Meredith for that matter. Therefore, I only have one option.

My voice steadies. "And I've been thinking about that... about what you *might* have seen on the security footage... It would probably take a large chunk of change to hire a big-time lawyer and to get your brothers and sisters out of Mexico and into the States legally."

Her brow cocks with interest.

Emboldened, I press on. "You know... if Emilia suddenly finds herself the recipient of a large payout, I could talk to her.

Or maybe I could find a way to transfer the funds myself, without her ever knowing."

Consuelo doesn't react immediately, but I don't need to elaborate. We both know what I'm offering: a piece of Thomas's life insurance policy in return for her secrecy. Blood money.

A pair of headlights sweep across the room.

The police are here.

Consuelo and I stare at each other, my pulse thudding in my ears.

Car doors slam. Boots on the ground.

"You're right," she says finally, the corner of her lip tugging upward. "It would take a large chunk of change, Lucy."

SIXTY-TWO

JAMES

Now

Thomas's body was discovered the following morning, his remains scattered at the base of the ravine. What the scavengers hadn't torn apart, the elements had worked to erase. Thomas's face, his hands—most of his exposed skin—had been ripped away, leaving behind a gruesome tableau that ensured no one would linger long enough to look closer. The police are still waiting on the dental records to confirm the identity, but everyone knows it's Thomas. There's no doubt.

The news of Thomas's death was quickly leaked. The town gossips wove their own stories. They said Thomas had been crumbling for years, a man hollowed out by the weight of caring for his sick wife. Losing Meredith—the woman everyone now understood had been his mistress—was the final blow. They said Thomas didn't fall at all—he jumped.

Everything went according to plan. But an unexpected hurdle arose when the chief of police questioned whether Emilia was mentally stable enough to sign the documentation required to finalize her husband's passing (cremation, death certificates, etc.), including transferring their accounts into her name. Because I—*James*, not Lucy—was considered legally deceased by the state, Thomas had no other next of kin to handle his postmortem affairs. And I definitely wasn't going to reveal my identity now. It would raise too much suspicion.

Emilia didn't waver. Calm, composed, she urged the police to call a physician for an evaluation. A doctor came to the house and vouched for my mother without hesitation. Emilia, he assured them, understood exactly what she was doing. She was in full control of her faculties, capable of making decisions independently, and was not being influenced by anyone else. That sealed it. Emilia was deemed fit to act as guardian of the Caine estate, now that her husband was deceased.

The documents were signed, one after another, her hand steady through it all. With Thomas gone, everything transferred to her: the estate, the accounts, and a hefty life-insurance payout.

Emilia is scheduled to begin physical therapy next week. In six to eight months, she should be fully rehabilitated, stronger than she's been in years.

And just like that, we got away with murder.

But did we?

It's one o'clock in the morning. The night is crystal-clear and unseasonably cold. I'm sitting in Emilia's armchair, staring listlessly into the dark forest below. She's asleep in bed. A crescent moon hangs above the treetops. Above it, a million stars twinkle in an endless black sky.

I'm drunk.

I've not spoken to Consuelo since the police visited the first time. Since I *blackmailed* her. I stay upstairs with Emilia, and Consuelo has officially moved in downstairs, knowing full-well I won't kick her out because of what she knows. She has me under her thumb and I don't like it. It feels like she's slipped into Thomas's role.

I *don't* like it.

When I told Emilia that Consuelo knows what we did, Emilia didn't hesitate in agreeing to offering a large lump sum to ensure her discretion in the matter. I knew she'd do it. We've come too far now.

I twirl the amber liquid around in my glass.

Consuelo is a loose end.

She must be dealt with.

I take a long sip, allowing the whiskey to burn its way down my throat. Closing my eyes, I ask myself the same questions I've asked a hundred times.

Did Consuelo kill her boyfriend, Marcus Alvarez? Did she kill Meredith? I know there is no way I can prove she killed Marcus, so figuring out if she killed Meredith is my only hope. I *need* to know. I need something more than blood money because what would stop her from coming back, time after time, asking for more money than we offered?

No. That can't happen.

I down my drink, rise from the armchair, and quietly enter the hallway.

The house is quiet.

Careful to avoid the creaking floorboards, I sneak down the hall, past the library, and into the media room. Using every tool I can find, I try for what feels like an hour to pick those damn locks that lead to the security hub.

No luck.

I decide to try one more place.

The door at the end of the hall creaks as I open it.

Goosebumps prickle my arms as I scan the dozens of pictures of my old self—James—tacked to the walls. From infancy to high school, the boy I hated—the boy I didn't understand—is everywhere. The newspaper articles, interviews, illegible handwritten notes, they all make my head spin and stomach sink.

I'm not this person anymore. I am Lucy. I like Lucy.

I force myself to focus on the reason for the visit. Emilia's old computer is the only one I haven't checked for access to the security system. If I can find footage of Consuelo drugging Meredith, I have my leverage.

As I lower onto the chair, the whiskey catches up with me and the room begins to spin. I close my eyes, focus on my feet on the ground.

Sweat beads over my skin.

I am *really* drunk.

I take several deep breaths. Once I've regained my footing, I power up the system.

Password?

Chewing my lower lip, I lean in, knowing I only have three attempts until I'm locked out. What would Emilia have as her password? Something she loves?

I type: *ITALY.*

Nope.

I type her mother's name: *GIUSEPPA*

Nope.

One more try.

The chubby, ruddy cheeks of my first-grade picture smiles back at me.

I type: *JAMES*

The screen lights and programs begin to populate the space. I'm in.

It takes a few minutes to orient myself to the desktop. There are at least two dozen folders, and double that of images and saved web pages. Everything is labeled, in organized folders. Most everything relates to my disappearance.

I frown, wondering what the name of the security company Thomas used is. I bring up the browser and type *home security companies near me* into the search engine. The screen populates. I check each folder, but none correlate to any of the local companies.

I try Emilia's Gmail account but am locked out after three failed password attempts. I could check Thomas's credit card statements, assuming the security fee is automatically deducted each month, but that would take forever. And I wouldn't know where to find the statements, anyway.

I begin clicking through files.

Ten minutes, thirty minutes, an hour passes.

I am about to give up when I click on an icon that, I hadn't realized, stores all the apps in once place.

Bingo—1st Choice System Security.

I click into the app, which brings up a slew of options. I click on "Cameras."

My pulse begins to quicken as I scan the long list. Each camera has its own folder labeled with the location, and inside the folder contains an identification number for each camera at that location. There are *hundreds*.

After clicking into a few, I learn that each camera records on twelve-hour loops. Once twelve hours pass, the file is saved into the app, accessible via a secure link, and then the recording erases from the camera and begins recording anew.

"What are you doing, Lucy?"

I jump and spin around in the chair.

Consuelo stands in the doorway.

SIXTY-THREE
JAMES

Now

I swallow the knot in my throat. "You scared me."

Consuelo studies the security cameras on the screen, then settles her gaze on me.

The hair on the back of my neck prickles. *Warning, warning, warning.*

I glance over her shoulder at the doorway. There's no way I can get past her and make a break for it.

"What are you doing?" she asks again, her voice low and accusatory.

"Nothing, I—"

"You still think I did it, don't you? You think I killed Meredith. And you're looking for proof so that you'll have more than just money to blackmail me with. Isn't that right?" She crosses her arms over her chest.

Whiskey-fueled anger mixes with the adrenaline. "Yeah, that's right. Busted. Because yeah, Consuelo, I do think you killed Meredith."

"Why?"

"Because she was a bitch who had dirt on you. You hated her."

"You mean she was a bitch who blackmailed me, like you?"

"I'm not a bitch. After all, I didn't set my boyfriend on fire."

For the first time, Consuelo's tough exterior wavers. She didn't expect that curveball. I watch as she hesitates, weighing how to wade into this new game between us.

I press in. "Your abusive boyfriend's home was burned down during your time off. Did you forget you told me his name? I saw the news story."

Consuelo's eyes round.

My confidence skyrockets. I stand from the chair, too wired to remain seated. "I saw you loading up Thomas's gas cans in the back of your car the *day before* Marcus died in the fire. I thought it was weird. The night you came back, I took the binoculars and peered down at your car, looking for the cans. What I saw was all your belongings loaded in your backseat. Tell me how you had the foresight to pack up all your clothes and toiletries *before* your boyfriend's house burned down?"

She opens her mouth, but I cut her off.

"You said you took a road trip that weekend. Let me guess, you created a trail of hotel check-ins to cover your tracks."

"You don't have proof."

"I have pictures, Consuelo," I lie. "Of you loading up the gas cans, and then later, of your stuff in the backseat."

She's speechless.

"Just come clean, Consuelo. You killed them both. Marcus and Meredith."

"I didn't kill Meredith!" She hisses. "Yes, I hated her. But she had enough demons. She never hurt me, like Marcus did. I had no reason to do anything to her other than to stay out of her way. She was a drunk and an addict, and she'd finally had enough of Thomas's lies. Honestly? I'm not surprised the way it ended."

"But it is a surprise how your boyfriend's life ended."

"Fine. *Lucy.*" Consuelo exhales sharply. "From one killer to another, *yes*, I killed my abusive boyfriend. *I did it.* Okay?"

She begins pacing, fists clenched at her sides. "Marcus *lied* to me. He *manipulated* me—just like Thomas did to Emilia. It went on for years. And he'd beaten me for even longer." She pauses and squeezes her eyes shut, as if she can still feel his hands on her.

When she opens her eyes again, they gleam with something raw. "After I saw what Thomas and Meredith did to Emilia, I got so *angry*—at them, at men like them, at all the sick bastards who get away with it." Her voice rises. "Something had to be *done!*"

I nod, truly understanding.

"So I made a plan," she continues, voice tight. "And I did it. I was going to bury Thomas, too, with the evidence I copied, but *you* got there first." A mirthless, breathy chuckle escapes her lips. She shakes her head, rubbing her temples.

"And, yes, that's exactly what I did—I checked into several hotels to make sure I had a trail and an alibi. But even if I hadn't covered my tracks, no one knew I was living there. Marcus had no real friends here, just people from work who barely spoke to him. His *real* friends are back in Mexico, and you think the cops would go searching for them? *Please.*"

Her lips press into a tight, bitter line. "I packed my things while Marcus was passed out drunk on the couch. Then I lit the place on fire. Every trace of me burned down with that house." She stares at me, her dark eyes unwavering.

Then, finally, she exhales a slow, measured breath.

"There. Are you *happy* now?" She jabs a finger at me. "Your turn. Why did you help Emilia kill Thomas?"

I want to divulge my true identity. But it's too fresh, still too risky.

But this answer isn't a lie. "Because I understand how it

feels to live life in a cage. To feel like no matter what you do, you can't get away."

A long moment stretches between us.

"I guess we all do." Consuelo says finally, glancing at the ceiling where Emilia's room is.

Tears fill our eyes. We both take long, deep inhales.

"Well, I guess this puts us in a precarious place, doesn't it?" I say gently.

"It does. I know you helped Emilia kill Thomas, and you know I killed Marcus." She closes the inches between us. Tears spill down her cheeks as she raises her pinky finger, suggesting a truce.

"To death?"

I wrap my pinky around hers. "To death."

We embrace in a newly bonded sisterhood.

One of secrets.

SIXTY-FOUR

JAMES

Now

The next morning, I'm back behind the computer. I feel confident in the truce Consuelo and I made last night, but I won't rest until the footage of Emilia and me luring Thomas to his death is erased for good.

I click on the "Garden West" folder, the one that contains the cameras that face the ravine. Inside this file are hundreds of videos, organized by month and day.

I slow my scroll as the date of Meredith's death comes into view. Though this isn't what I'm looking for, before I can stop myself, I double click the file.

I find myself pausing.

Do I want to see it?

My mind says no, but the sick little voice in my head says yes.

Unfortunately, the camera doesn't give a clear view into the master bathroom window, where Meredith would have snuck in to steal Emilia's Xanax.

I squint, tapping my finger against the key. Where else could I see her that day?

I click into "Porch," hoping to get a shot into the guest bedroom where she died. No luck.

I click into "Patio East." As expected, the camera records the east side of the patio, which runs the length of the kitchen. The wall of windows offers a clear, unobstructed view into the kitchen.

I click on the same date, press play, lean back, and watch.

After fifteen minutes of nothing, I get bored and hit fast forward. I pause when I see Consuelo enter the kitchen. I watch as she refills her coffee, then leaves.

Time stamp: 11:17 a.m.

Two and a half hours later, at 1:58 p.m., Meredith enters the kitchen. After rummaging through the fridge, she selects a bottle of wine from the pantry. She pours a (ridiculously large) glass. She leaves the bottle on the counter, then disappears.

At 2:14 p.m. *Emilia* staggers into the room, unsteady, holding onto the wall for support. She's wearing the beige robe I dress her in during the daytime.

My jaw unhinges as I propel myself forward, inches from the screen. I gawk at my mother's image, my mind racing. This was *before* we'd begun weaning her medication. Was my mom more lucid than she'd led even me to believe?

Where was I? Why hadn't I seen her? I was probably either napping, or showering, or perhaps outside on a walk. I can't remember. Either way, there she is. And I had *no* idea.

Heart pounding, I watch as *my mother* picks up the bottle of wine Meredith had opened earlier, and studies the label. She's obviously very drugged and lethargic as it takes her a few seconds to register what her eyes are scanning—but she does it. She sets it back down, then stumbles out the room, her legs almost giving out on her twice.

2:37 p.m.: Meredith enters, refills her wine glass, then disappears.

3:29 p.m.: Meredith enters again, refills her glass. Disappears.

3:34 p.m.: Consuelo passes by the room, carrying a bag of gardening tools.

I click to the garden camera and watch as Consuelo settles in on the far east of the property to do yard work. Just like she said she'd done.

I click back to the kitchen.

4:42 p.m.: Emilia, *my mother*, re-enters, stumbling even more than before. I watch as she checks over her shoulder, then makes her way to the bottle of wine that is certainly almost empty by now.

Emilia retrieves a small plastic bag from her robe pocket.

I watch as she pours the powdery white contents into the wine bottle that Meredith is drinking from.

I watch her replace the cork and leave the room.

My pulse roars in my ears as I stare at the paused image of my mother pouring what I know is crushed Xanax into Meredith's bottle of wine.

SIXTY-FIVE
EMILIA

Now

There's one secret I've kept from James: I was the one who poisoned Meredith—just like she had done to me for years. Also, that there were days that I was far more lucid than he—or anyone—had dared to believe. And in those stolen moments of clarity, I plotted. Not just the murder of my husband, Thomas, but of Meredith as well.

The plans had unfurled slowly, like the curling edges of an old photograph, darkening with time. At first, it had been nothing more than a vague dream—a fleeting thought born of desperation. But desperation, when left unchecked, can become something far more dangerous.

Each day in that house, I gathered scraps of information, observed routines, and tested the limits of their arrogance. They never saw me coming.

I had originally intended to bring Consuelo into my plan—loyal, watchful Consuelo with much to lose. She would have been the perfect accomplice. But when Lucy—my son, James—returned, it felt as though fate had set the board. James had his own reasons to loathe Thomas, his own ghosts to exorcise. That battle, I knew, had to belong to him—and I would help, of course.

Meredith, though? She was mine. My trash to take out. My wrong to right.

Once all the pieces of the puzzle were finally coming together, I took my chance. While James was having a nap, I crept downstairs, my footsteps light, my pulse hammering so loudly I feared it would betray me. Half expecting to be caught, I moved through the shadows, ready to spin some fragile excuse if necessary. But no one stopped me.

When I saw Meredith in the kitchen, it felt like the universe was handing me a gift. She stood at the counter, wine bottle open, her back turned, utterly unaware.

It was too perfect.

The years she had spent poisoning me were over. That day I finally returned the favor.

My dirty little secret that I will take to my grave.

I have no regrets.

Only the sharp, intoxicating taste of revenge.

SIXTY-SIX
EMILIA

Eight Months Later

I stand at the edge of Piazza San Marco, clutching my coat against the gentle chill drifting off the lagoon. The square hums with life—tourists laughing and snapping photos, pigeons fluttering in lazy circles. The lilting music of Venetian dialects weaves through the air like a song I'm beginning to understand—to remember.

The slick cobblestone streets reflect the twinkling lights of the restaurants, and the air is ripe with recent rain. I lower my umbrella, a cheerful yellow against the muted grays of the city, and continue my stroll along the bustling streets.

I'm not in a rush. This city has taught me the beauty of wandering without purpose.

After James and I sold the glass house, we said goodbye to Thomas, to the past, to all our mistakes, and we both took that first, very scary step into the next phase of our lives.

Into the unknown.

When I first arrived in Italy, I was overwhelmed. My Italian was clumsy, my confidence shaky, and everything—from finding an apartment to ordering an espresso—felt like a battle. But now, months later, I see the city through new eyes. I'm beginning to remember the rhythm of it, the way it breathes.

The apartment I struggled to find has become my sanctuary. I've filled the space with soft blankets, twinkling lights, and the smell of fresh basil from a plant on the windowsill. It's small, but it's mine. Every morning, I wake to the sound of the motorboats humming through the canals, the distant chime of church bells.

Every morning, I smile.

There's a lightness in my chest now, a freedom I never thought I'd feel again. For so long, my life was a series of careful compromises, of tiptoeing around Thomas's demands and watching my own dreams shrink to fit within the walls he built around me. But here—here, I am untethered. I decide where I go, what I eat, who I speak to, even what time I get out of bed.

Every step through the narrow streets of Venice feels like an act of defiance, a reclaiming of something I lost. I've started taking long walks without a destination, simply letting the city guide me. I wander over bridges, past faded façades and windows framed by flower boxes, letting the golden light of the canals wrap around me like a warm embrace. I belong here, in this city that feels timeless and alive all at once.

I waited for weeks to connect with my distant relatives. Perhaps because I didn't know who I was anymore, so how could I handle the emotional weight of forging a connection with someone else? For so long, I'd been under Thomas's control, confined to that bedroom like a forgotten relic. Before I could face them, I needed time to breathe, to remember what it meant to exist on my own terms.

My mother, Giuseppa, however, is never far from my thoughts. My memory of her—our time together here in Italy—now feels more like a connection than a memory. I find her in the simplest things: the smell of garlic sizzling in olive oil, the golden light spilling over the canals at sunset, the bustling markets so filled with life.

I turn my face to the lagoon, breathe in the wind on my cheek.

In the soft thrum of the distant music, Mother's words come back to me: *"La vita è come il vino, cara. Ci vuole tempo per farlo buono." Life is like wine, my dear. It takes time to make it good.*

And now, I understand. My life isn't something to wait for or endure—it's something to savor, to create, to fill with every ounce of joy and beauty I can find.

Turning a corner, I spot a small café tucked into an alcove, its golden light pooling onto the wet street. The soft clink of glasses and quiet laughter drift from inside.

I almost pass it by, but something deep inside my soul, a gentle tug, pulls me to it.

Stepping inside, I shake out my umbrella and glance around. The café is intimate, with only a handful of tables. A wood-burning fireplace crackles in the corner, casting flickering shadows on the walls.

I spot an empty seat by the window, and I make my way over.

That's when I see him.

A lone man seated at the bar, his broad shoulders wrapped in a dark, tailored coat. As if sensing my gaze, he turns slightly, revealing a profile so striking it takes me a moment to look away. Dark hair, damp from the rain, curls slightly at the edges. A strong jawline softened by a hint of stubble. He lifts a glass of red wine to his lips, his movements unhurried, deliberate.

I settle into my seat, willing myself not to stare. But as fate would have it, he has noticed me.

The waiter approaches. I order a glass of wine. The man turns fully now, studying me with a curiosity that sends butter-flies fluttering through my stomach. His eyes are a deep, stormy gray, and he has a slight dimple when he smiles and raises his glass in a silent toast.

I nod back, blushing through a smile.

My heart skitters, and I feel like a giddy schoolgirl, as he stands and walks toward my table.

"Scusi," he says, his voice smooth, his Italian lilting with the faintest hint of something else—French, maybe? "Do you mind if I join you?"

I gesture to the empty chair across from me. "Not at all. Please."

"I'm Mathieu," he says, leaning back in his seat, his gaze steady but kind. "You're not from here, are you?"

"Emilia," I reply, feeling confident for the first time in years. "I was born and raised here, but left when I was young." I smile. "Now I'm back."

We fall into easy, flirty conversation. As each minute passes, I feel more and more comfortable, like we lived in a different life together. Like this moment—this man—was something the city had been waiting to show me all along.

The night stretches on, our conversation winding through stories of travel, art, and the strange beauty of Venice in the rain. When we finally part, exchanging promises to meet again, I step back into the drizzle with a feeling I haven't had in years: hope. The kind that doesn't just flicker but burns steady and bright, warming me from the inside out.

I glance at my watch.

I need to get going. I have an early flight to Atlanta.

SIXTY-SEVEN
JAMES

Eight Months Later

After Emilia made the long journey back to Italy, I moved to Atlanta to get a real job. A real, grown-up office job with a bi-weekly paycheck I could depend on. Something that guaranteed that I would never, ever live in my Tahoe again.

I made the move as James—not Lucy, the persona I'd created to escape and survive—because I didn't need to survive anymore. I wanted to be the version of me that might have existed if life had taken a different path. I wanted to give him a shot. A "life do-over" as my mother would call it.

This new version of James—sharp-suited, clean-shaven, professional—fit neatly into the corporate world. But deep down, I craved something else entirely. I wanted to stand in front of an easel, my sleeves rolled up and my hands smeared with paint. That's where I felt alive—where I felt real. Painting wasn't just an outlet for me; it was who I was.

I'd painted almost every night since moving to Atlanta, and I'd even sold a few pieces through a local online retailer. It wasn't much, but it was something.

Months later, an unexpected opportunity forced me to confront the gap between the two parts of myself. One of my paintings from the online shop—an abstract piece capturing the auras of a crowd—caught the eye of a local gallery owner. She wanted to feature the painting—and me—in an upcoming show.

The idea terrified me, but I said yes.

On the evening of the event, I stepped onto the stage, the spotlight cutting through the dimly lit room. The audience was filled with artists and enthusiasts, people who saw me as a painter, an artist, a storyteller. But in the front row, I spotted my boss, Laura, and one of my senior colleagues from work.

My nerves exploded. They weren't supposed to see the artist side of me. I felt exposed, like an actor caught out of costume.

I began my talk hesitantly, explaining the emotions and stories behind my paintings. My voice trembled at first, but as I kept speaking, something shifted. The audience wasn't judging me—they were listening. Connecting.

Somewhere mid-way, I allowed myself to disclose my ability to see auras. By the time I finished, the applause was overwhelming. For the first time in months, I felt like I belonged.

Afterward, Laura approached me, smiling warmly.

"Why didn't you tell me you were this talented?" she asked.

I hesitated, then said, "I didn't think it was... professional. I thought I had to keep that part of me separate."

She shook her head. "Professionalism isn't about hiding who you are. It's about bringing your whole self to the table. That's what makes people stand out."

Her words stayed with me long after the event.

Soon, colleagues I barely knew began opening up, sharing their own creative passions and hidden talents. For the first time, I didn't feel like I was living a double life. I was just... living.

The day I sold a painting to a major gallery while also

receiving a promotion at work felt surreal. I no longer had to choose between James and Lucy. They were... me.

That evening, I stood on the balcony of my apartment, a glass of wine in one hand and a paintbrush in the other. The city lights shimmered against the night sky, and for the first time in a long time, I felt whole. Not fractured. Not divided between two people. Just... me.

Then the phone rang. It was the gallery owner. She wanted to host a full exhibition of my work.

The gallery hums with quiet anticipation, the air thick with the scent of fresh paint. My first solo art exhibit. It feels surreal. The walls are lined with pieces that are as much a part of me as my own breath. Paintings that reflect years of struggle, growth, and discovery. Not only from my time here in Atlanta, from my days as Lucy in Los Angeles. It's *all* there—me, in every way, shape, and form. Tonight, I'm exposing not only my work, but myself, every layer peeled back and laid bare for strangers to see.

I'm unbelievably nervous. My suit feels tighter than it should, the collar of my white dress shirt like a noose.

I glance at the clock. Fifteen minutes until the doors open, and already sweat is beginning to form under my suit. The gallery owner claps me on the shoulder, her voice warm and encouraging. "You've got this, James. People are going to love it."

I nod, managing a smile, but inside, doubt gnaws at me.

The first guests trickle in—gallery regulars, art enthusiasts, a few colleagues from work. They study the pieces with thoughtful expressions, murmuring to one another as the room begins to fill. I'm doing my best to stay composed, to mingle and answer questions about my work, when the door swings open, and I see her.

Emilia.

My mother—absolutely glowing—steps inside slowly, her eyes scanning the room until they land on me. My heart stops. I haven't seen her in months, not since she moved back to Italy to rebuild her life. But here she is, elegant and composed, her gray coat draped over her shoulders and her white-blonde hair swept back in a way that reminds me of when I was a boy.

"Mom?" I manage, the word barely more than a whisper.

Her smile lights the room. "You didn't think I'd miss this, did you?"

I cross the room in a few long strides, pulling her into a hug. I smell her perfume, her hair—*her*.

"I can't believe you came all this way," I step back to study her.

"I wanted it to be a surprise." Her gaze moves across the walls. "I'm so proud of you, James. This is... incredible."

I don't know what to say. My mother's approval means more to me than I'd realized, and for the first time tonight, I feel a flicker of calm. Of everything being exactly as it should be.

Before I can catch my breath, the door opens again, and a familiar voice calls out. "Well, don't get too emotional. You've got more surprises coming."

I turn to see Consuelo, standing just inside the gallery with a group behind her. Her brothers and sisters, here from Mexico, and on their way to American citizenship.

"Consuelo," I say, smiling so big it hurts my cheeks.

She grins. "*James*. Good to see you."

I glance over my shoulder at Emilia, who winks, and I realize they've spoken before tonight, and that Emilia must have told Consuelo who I really am. The relief hits harder than expected.

No more secrets! No more faking. Not for anyone, not ever, ever again. It feels like an incredible weight has been lifted off my shoulders.

"You didn't have to come," I say, overwhelmed.

"Of course I did." Her eyes sparkle. "We're family. Come, meet everyone."

After introductions have been made, the room feels smaller, warmer, filled with the kind of connection I've been searching for all along.

The night unfolds in a way I couldn't have imagined. Emilia drifts from painting to painting, her expressions shifting between pride and quiet reflection. Consuelo does the same, pointing out details in my work to her brothers and sisters.

As the evening winds down, I find myself standing in the corner with Emilia and Consuelo.

Three survivors. Bound by blood (and maybe a little blackmail).

With not a single regret.

Emilia holds a glass of wine, her posture relaxed in a way that feels new, lighter. Consuelo leans against the wall, her arms crossed, a small smile tugging at her lips.

I glance around the room, at the paintings, the people, the connections being made, at the people who see me for who I truly am.

James.

Consuelo raises her glass in a mock toast. "To James, the artist," she says, her grin widening. "And to surprises."

"To surprises," Emilia echoes, her glass clinking softly against mine.

"To being who we are truly meant to be," I add, realizing that this moment is everything I've been working toward. Not just as an artist or a professional, but as myself. Whole, grounded, and finally happy.

A LETTER FROM THE AUTHOR

Dear Readers – let's stay in touch!
Sign up here to hear about my new releases with Storm:

www.stormpublishing.co/amanda-mckinney

Sign up here to be included in my personal newsletter:

www.amandamckinneyauthor.com/contact

If you enjoyed *The Wife's Silence* and could spare a few moments to leave a review that would be hugely appreciated. Even a short review can make all the difference in encouraging a reader to discover my books for the first time. Thank you so much!

facebook.com/AmandaMcKinneyAuthor
instagram.com/amandamckinneyauthor
tiktok.com/amandamckinneyauthor

ACKNOWLEDGMENTS

Dear Readers,

I want to take a moment to thank you, from the bottom of my heart.

If you follow me on social media, you know that my life took an abrupt and heartbreaking turn in 2024, when we lost our beautiful ten-year-old son to mitochondrial disease.

During the four weeks we were in the ICU, I wrote. (In fact, I was writing this very book.) Each day since, I write. Writing has always been a place of refuge for me—an escape from the world—but in these past months, it's been so much more. It's been survival.

And I would not have this lifeline without you.

Thank you for reading my books, for your continued support, and well wishes. For giving me the gift of continuing to do what I love, even in the darkest of times. You are an invaluable part of my life, and I will never stop being grateful.

Love,

Amanda

www.ingramcontent.com/pod-product-compliance
Lightning Source LLC
Chambersburg PA
CBHW010434170726
48283CB00011B/3199

"Surreal and Magical. Your book pulls me in and out of
the present and I fall into your drawings as if I am inside
the dream. Your words flow like water or a steady beating
drum. And all colour evaporates, it's just 'chiaroscuro',
contrasting light and shadows. It's like being asleep and
being woken with a phrase or command that suddenly
causes you to remember…. Everything! It's beautiful."

"A spellbinding homage to the daughter of a Selkie,
Kelsey Ashe continues to mesmerize across this
ecological allegory. Her exquisitely illustrated Deep Green
Sea will ferry readers off to Avalon. Imagine the break of
Hokusai's wave in the chambers of a surrealist grotto. Or
beach-combing Angela Carter's "new wine in old bottles"
on an Antipodean shore."

"The Deep Green Sea is a challenging and mind-bending
tale that commands profound self-introspection. Both a
questing adventure and spiritual journey, the story
accounts for times in our lives when everything is turned
completely upside down by grief or traumatic
circumstance. Equally harrowing as it is beautiful, the
otherworldly setting Ashe has created is full of strong
female characters who forge on through every setback."

"This exquisite book ignites the imagination in ways I could not have predicted, encouraging pause for thought and inviting deep reflection. It had me aching one minute and elated the next. If it were possible to live inside a painting and a poem all at once, this is the place. It feels almost channelled and entwined with real life and a higher realm. My mind was exercised within an inch, with imagery so rich, raw and vivid."
Anastasia Carlson: Dramaturge & Live Storyteller, Perth, Western Australia.

"What a story. I was taken on such a trip. The journey you take the reader on is a metaphor for life, filled with pain and suffering, redemption but ultimately one of love. A journey we all take…woven it into a surreal story, a world of powerful women, of wonder. It is a rare jewel that can lay their soul bare, with such honesty, beauty and grace, embracing the chaos of life to weave a story so wonderful. You have captured something magical."
Jim Cable: Artist. Fremantle, Western Australia.

"The Deep Green Sea is a deeply mystical tale of life and death, birth and rebirth, and the path we walk as celestial beings between worlds. The journey of Roe, Orla, and the many guides who make part of their story come alive, provides the reader with a rich account of what it means to accept our light and fear, to know how destiny and fate shape our human journey, and the understanding that our power resides deep within our own soul."
Claire Falcon: Author, Psychic Medium, Intuition Teacher. Berlin, Germany.

"An absolutely captivating tale. It is a timeless, archetypal journey that resonates so deeply. Amazingly immersive…with its vivid word-scapes and windswept artwork, this story had me spellbound."
Edward Sparks: Author, *The Glow*.
Perth, Western Australia.

"Lush and Haunting. A tale as mysterious and mesmerising as the sea. For lovers of fairytales, mythology, the surreal and magical. Kelsey Ashe's lyrical words shimmer in the liminal space of dreams and memory. Kelsey, a word and art witch, has cast a glistening magic charm which, like all fairy tales, will help you transcend life challenges as you submerge into the underworld of her fantastical deep green sea."
Josephine Pennicott: Author, *The Circle of Nine* Dark Fantasy Trilogy, *Poet's Cottage* and *Currawong Manor*. Blue Mountains, NSW, Australia.

In Orla's words "it made my breath skip". Ashe writes in intoxicating ebbs and flows, as if she is writing from the seabed itself. The Deep Green Sea casts a peculiar and watery spell over you. There's a surreal luminosity to Ashe's futuristic world-building, whilst she traverses myth, allegory and contemporary ecological thinking with poetic touch. Spend time on this novella; in the words of Ashe; "all departures can be delayed".
Molly Gilroy: Editor/Co-Founder *The Debutante Feminist Surrealist Journal*. Edinburgh, Scotland, United Kingdom.